Time to Decide

Riding to Colorado to investigate a shipment of doctored silver ingots, Trey Cormac comes across a robbery. Scattering the bandits and saving a hostage is what any professional bounty hunter would do, but nothing is quite what it seems. At twenty-five and slightly inexperienced, he lets himself be sweet-talked by a pretty young woman, which lands him in a whole load of trouble. Embarrassed at being such a gullible target, Trey sets out to restore his self-respect. But chasing after the young woman only draws him in deeper. Framed and friendless, he is left to face a hostile jury and a hanging judge. Could things get any worse? Probably.

Time to Decide

Frank Chandler

A Black Horse Western

ROBERT HALE

© Frank Chandler 2019
First published in Great Britain 2019

ISBN 978-0-7198-3055-6

The Crowood Press
The Stable Block
Crowood Lane
Ramsbury
Marlborough
Wiltshire SN8 2HR

www.bhwesterns.com

Robert Hale is an imprint
of The Crowood Press

Typeset by
Derek Doyle & Associates, Shaw Heath
Printed and bound in Great Britain by
4Bind Ltd, Stevenage, SG1 2XT

1

Trey Cormac ran up the steps to the sheriff's office, tripped and crashed through the door, falling headlong across the floorboards. The three men in the office broke off their conversation and stared at the sprawled figure. Shamefaced, Trey got to his feet, dusted himself off and smiled.

'That's quite an entrance, young man,' the sheriff remarked.

'A bit too keen,' added the deputy.

Trey picked up his hat and held it awkwardly in front of himself, twisting the brim between his fingers.

The deputy eased the situation. 'Coffee?'

The sheriff introduced himself and his deputy. The third man in the office was a federal marshal. Trey explained that he was a bounty hunter and although only twenty-five had proved himself with his gun and now he wanted a job as a sheriff's deputy.

'How did you know I was one short?' the sheriff wondered.

'I heard,' Trey said simply. 'Someone told me there

was a job going in Corburg.'

'Well, it's true,' the sheriff agreed. 'I need another one, but you're a bit too young for a responsibility like that. Where d'you come from anyway?'

'Atherton.'

The deputy frowned. 'That's a hundred miles from here. Why not work somewhere nearer your home.'

Trey breathed in heavily and ran his fingers through his thick black hair, his eyes distant. 'My folks passed a while back, nowhere's home. Give me a chance, you'll not regret it.'

The sheriff looked mildly interested. 'How much have you earned as a bounty hunter, sonny?'

'A couple of thousand.'

The deputy laughed. 'And you think this job pays more!'

'No, but it's regular money and maybe I could settle for a while. Been on the road too long.'

The sheriff shook his head. 'Listen son, take my advice, twenty-five just ain't the right age to be settling down. Have you been sowing seeds, got a girl in trouble?'

Trey pretended to be shocked. 'No, sir, I have not!'

The deputy smirked and was about to say something, but the sheriff held up his hand to stop him. He opened a drawer on his desk and took out a couple of papers. He passed them across to Trey.

'Tell you what I'll do, have a look at that. You can read, can't you?'

Trey nodded and scanned the two pages. It was a handwritten letter complaining about some suspicious silver bars that had been received by one of the town's banks against a bill of exchange. Trey frowned.

'Guess you don't quite follow,' the sheriff said.

'No, I don't,' Trey agreed. 'What's the problem?'

The sheriff stood up. 'The silver bars have been doctored, the bank realized too late they weren't pure, there was too much variation in the weight of the bars. Even allowing for a bit of error in the casting, they didn't feel right. The bank had one drilled and it contained lead as well as silver.'

The marshal took over. 'The problem is these bars have come from way out west, a crooked little operation in Colorado probably. They look good, they're stamped proper, but we made some enquiries and nobody can trace the exact plant they came from. There ain't no smelting business with the name on the bars, Casey & Co. It's a simple swindle on a massive scale. The bars were deposited here by a merchant, who has since disappeared. The bank is paying a handsome reward for any useful information because they're out by many thousands of dollars.'

'And you want me to find out about it?'

The sheriff intervened. 'That's up to you, son, but if you do you'll get a hefty reward from the bank and I'll consider you for a job as a deputy. What d'you say?'

Trey's eyes lit up with the prospect. 'Sounds like a fair deal.'

The marshal issued words of warning. 'Listen, young man, this isn't some petty criminal you're after, this isn't a two hundred dollar bounty job, this is darned serious federal business and there's a good chance you'll get yourself killed. Think carefully before you take this on. All we're after is information, then we'll get a legal process to take care of it.'

The sheriff nodded.

'The marshal's right. Downright dangerous. Think it over. 'Course if you'd rather do somethin' else I've got a pile of two-bit dodgers with all sorts of chicken feed that need to be brought in.'

Trey got up quietly. 'Thank you, sir, my mind is already made up. How far is Colorado?'

The sheriff took Trey to a map on the wall and jabbed it with his finger. 'We're here, Corburg, marked with the red dot. Way over there close to those mountains is Denver. That'd be a good place to start looking. You sure you're up to this, sonny?'

'I'm sure.'

'Well then, there's one thing you could do to prove it. Yesterday the bank sent some of the bars as part of a shipment with the Corburg Transportation company in a stagecoach bound for one of their branches in a place called Copps Creek, that's several days' drive for a coach. That was before they realized the bars had been doctored. My deputy here was going to go after it, but if you want the job, go and find that coach and get the driver to bring it back with the silver. There's also bags of paper money too, so don't frighten the driver into thinking it's a hold-up. The guard's travelling inside the coach to avoid attracting bandits. If you succeed, the marshal will give you a letter of authorization to make enquiries for the source of these darned bars.'

8

*

It was less than half an hour since Trey had entered the sheriff's office, rather ignominiously, but he was leaving with a glint in his eye, his head held high, and his spirits almost at the same level. This was just the kind of break he'd been hoping for. Not exactly as good as being a deputy but it stirred his sense of adventure. With a bit of luck and hard riding he'd catch up with that coach.

He swung himself up into the saddle of his handsome black mustang, which, not given to sentimentality, he called Hoss, a fine beast with a spirit to match his own, and stamina to cross miles of rough country without a murmur of complaint. He'd bought it with the reward from his first bounty payment and was proud of it. The dealer had tried to sell him a sturdy quarter horse, but Trey wanted something fast, nimble and able to maintain long distances, the essential qualities of a bounty hunter's mount.

'Well, Hoss, we've got lots to do, a job in Denver finding Casey & Co, but first we've got to find a stagecoach, so we'd best get goin'.'

He pressed his heels lightly into the horse's flanks. 'On you go, and if I forget, we're going to Copps Creek.'

They trotted briskly along Main Street. The sun was near its zenith and the shadows were at their shortest. A light breeze was all that moved the stifling midday air. Few folk were about, most being inside for dinner or cooling off in the several saloons. Coming to the end of the town limit, Trey pulled up and swung round in his saddle to look back down the street. The name board had a few bullet holes, witness to high-spirited target practice; two had gone clean through the O of CORBURG and one each in the circles of the B and the two Rs. Trey doubted he could have shot that well himself and sincerely hoped he didn't come across the person who could.

For a moment, though, he imagined himself completing his tasks and proudly wearing the five-pointed star as a deputy sheriff of this thriving town of Corburg. He could see himself standing in the street, arms akimbo, legs apart, one hand near his holster facing down a desperate robber who would rather die fighting than be taken prisoner and hanged like a dog.

Hoss bucked and shook him out of the reverie.

'Easy up, critter. I know, I know. But, hey! A man's gotta have a dream.'

That night Trey pulled up at a little settlement that was barely more than a half dozen dwellings and a few scattered trading establishments, one of which was thankfully a saloon with a couple of rooms hired out to travellers. He secured oats and a stable for Hoss, a beef stew and thin mattress for himself and by the morning, both were pleased to be on their way once more.

After another day of hard riding he hadn't caught up with the coach. Stopping out for the night, he made a scrape in a water-cut ledge just above a dried up river bed. Hoss was hobbled and left to forage. Trey gathered up dead and broken branches, enough to make a fire, brew coffee and cook some beans and sausage. He had a smoke lying in his bedroll. Hoss was now tethered and only the cracking of the firewood spoilt the peace and quiet as nocturnal life began to emerge. Every now and then a small flurry of sparks would drift into the sky with the heat of the fire.

Next thing he knew, the sun was up, Hoss was standing silently, head bowed, one back leg bent as horses at rest will often do. The shadow of a vulture circling on an early morning thermal passed over the ground, but the bird saw nothing of interest and continued on its hunt for food. Much refreshed from a good night's sleep, Trey brewed some coffee, then kicked out the remains of the fire, gathered everything together and rode off, confident of catching up with the coach. Reaching the top of a ridge, he took out his telescope and scanned for any signs. The main commercial track was hidden where it ran along the valley, but there was a trail of dust. So he continued to ride parallel on the plateau, seeing it would cut off a big loop of road. With a bit of luck he'd drop down somewhere in front of the coach. His path now became thicker with trees, until the stunted pines slowed his progress to a slow walk.

Eventually it cleared. A light flurry of wind was just enough to stir the fresh green leaves on the clumps of aspens lining the valley and if he'd still been riding in the cover of the scrub under the twisted pines it is doubtful he'd have heard the gunfire. But he did, and it always made him tense with the memory of his first gunfight when he'd caught a pair of outlaws at their camp-fire. They drew on him, he shot one and winged the other. Having previously only tracked cows that had wandered off from his pa's herd, he was immensely proud of himself when he collected the bounty.

Since then he hadn't looked back and now called himself a professional bounty hunter with several scalps under his belt. But he really wanted to be a lawman, which is what had taken him to Corburg for the deputy's job. Being on a special mission to investigate these silver ingots thrilled him. It wasn't quite official, after all he didn't have the lawman's star yet, but the dream spurred him on.

Hearing the shots in the valley, he stopped his horse and listened carefully, fearing the worst. There were more gunshots, a few shouts and then it went quiet. He spurred his horse to the edge of the rim. It was a steep-sided scarp covered with patches of vegetation, mostly stunted trees clinging precariously with the slimmest of chances, trying not to be washed down in a rainstorm. At the foot of the slope the road ran a few feet above a raging river, bursting with the spring thaw. The tumbling white-flecked water racing over the boulders filled the valley with an ominous roar.

The foreground was an entirely different matter. Some three or four horses with mounted riders were circling the coach. The driver was prostrate on the bench, reins still in his hands. The limp body of the guard was sprawled on the ground, as dead as they come. A woman in city clothes standing by the coach door was being frisked for jewellery. Trey was still too far away to be effective but without further hesitation, he pulled his Winchester from the scabbard, levelled at one of the robbers and squeezed the trigger. The man immediately dropped his gun and clutched his arm. A lucky shot that made the other robbers look in his direction. The three of them quickly disengaged from the scene and rode off at full pelt, one of them turning in the saddle to loose off a bullet at the hapless woman. She fell to the ground with a scream. Another shot whistled somewhere near Trey's head, bringing down fragments of branch.

With a quick, experienced scan of the scarp, Trey picked out a way down to the road. For several minutes he was out of sight as his horse picked its way behind rocks and along narrow ledges, finally emerging a little way from the coach. The woman was still lying in the road. Trey swiftly dismounted.

'You all right, ma'am? Are you hit?'

She pulled herself up onto her knees and began to dust herself off, feeling carefully for any injury.

'Sonsofbitches!' she said, angrily. 'I'll see them swing for this. Taken my gold chain and two rings.'

She sat back on her heels and began to sob. 'My wedding ring and necklace. They just ripped it off me.'

Trey knelt down beside her. 'Well at least they left you with your life, good thing that last shot from the bandit was a wild one or I'd be speaking to a corpse. My name's Trey. Trey Cormac. I'm a bounty hunter and if there's anything I can do, just give me the word.

What's your name ma'am?'

She smiled warmly, tilting her head just a little. 'They call me Sherin.'

The way she said that told Trey all he needed to know. She wasn't a city lady, the wife of some wealthy merchant, more likely a chorus girl. She was indeed a rare beauty with shining coppery hair, green eyes and red lips, but he'd been with young ladies of that kind in some of the cow towns as he passed through, just to have a pleasant time and make the evenings a little less tedious, keeping him away from the poker tables. He'd learnt quite early that you lose your money both ways, and they can both be just as much fun or just as much pain.

'Were there any other travellers or just you?'

Sherin shrugged. 'Just me. The coach wasn't meant for passengers, the only cargo was a strong box. I think it was full of silver dollars on its way to some bank or other. They've lost it now anyway. I was in a hurry to get away from Corburg so I gave the driver some money to take me along, kinda hidden inside. Can you get me quickly to the next town?'

He lifted Sherin to her feet and dusted her down. 'This ride nearly cost you your life,' Trey observed. 'Luckily for you, I was looking for this coach.

The woman was taken aback. 'You were?'

'Yes, ma'am. It was on it's way to Copps Creek with a cargo of silver and cash, which I guess they've just stolen. I'd better take the coach to the next town and arrange for its return to Corburg. I'll have to drive it myself. Do you know how to hold a shot-gun?'

14

Sherin nodded. She walked over to the body of the guard and picked up the shot-gun that was lying by his side.

'We must get the bodies to the undertaker,' she said. 'Can't leave them here for wolves or vultures. It's only a few miles to the next town, Reeves Hope.'

Trey was surprised how composed Sherin seemed as they lifted the driver and guard into the coach and laid them down, one on each of the bench seats.

Sherin, holding the shot-gun, climbed up to the driving seat. Trey hitched his horse to the back of the coach, checked for damage to the pole, shafts, trees and harness and finally climbed up. He took hold of the reins and cajoled the two horses to continue the journey.

Prepared for anything, Trey now found himself in the unlikely position of coach driver. It was a job that didn't last long. They had only gone about three miles when Sherin told Trey to stop. He pulled up and put the brake on.

'Listen Trey,' she began, squinting into the sun. 'You might think this an odd request but, look, I said I was in a hurry to get away from that last place I stopped in, Corburg, and I was wondering if you'd be so kind as to do me another favour. I mean rescuing me like that was real kind. . . .'

'Spit it out, Sherin,' Trey said to interrupt the flow of words. 'What is it you want?'

'Well I was thinking if we just turn up like this with the coach an' all, there's goin' to be awkward questions with the sheriff in this next place, Reeves Hope.'

'I'll do the talking. I've been sent to get this coach anyway.'

'Yes, you said so,' she put her hand on Trey's arm. 'But listen, couldn't we just leave the coach here and tell the sheriff we think there's been a hold-up. He'll send a deputy to investigate. Otherwise there might be awkward questions. It might look like we robbed the coach, or you did. It'll save a lot of awkward questions.'

'What questions?'

'An' you and I could just ride into town, like husband and wife, on your horse, and it would save such a lot of difficulty.'

Trey threw his head back and laughed a good loud laugh. 'Are you joshing with me, ma'am! I'm a bounty hunter and this is my prize. I've got to get it back to Corburg whether there's any silver in it or not.'

Sherin bit her lip. 'Supposing I tell the sheriff you robbed the coach and brought me here as a hostage?'

'Why would you do that?'

'Try me. As a matter of fact, there's plenty of men would jump at the chance of taking me hostage!'

Trey was still chuckling when Sherin lifted her skirt and pulled a little gun from her garter.

'You sure I can't change your mind?'

2

Sherin waved the gun menacingly. Trey threw up his hands in a gesture of alarm. It was only a small pocket pistol but at that range it could do serious damage.

'Easy. Easy there, Sherin. Just you mind what you're doing with that thing and we can talk about it.'

'I want more than talk. You're a man of your word, I can see that. You're a good man actually. Just admit I've got the upper hand right now and say you'll ride me into town like your wife and I'll stand down.'

'What can I say, except yes?'

'Nothing unless you want a couple holes through your chest and out the other side.'

'Well, Sherin, I guess you're a kinda persuasive woman. So I'm going to say, you win. I'll ride you into town like husband and wife. Now put that little shooter back under your skirt.'

She did and Trey was as good as his word. Sherin wasn't much of a danger and she must have had a good reason to be fleeing from that other place. It wasn't Trey's concern. If he'd been in real danger he

17

was fairly sure he could have disarmed her before she managed to fire a shot, but there was no point. He'd never fought a woman and he didn't want to start now.

Calmly Trey unhitched his horse while Sherin collected her small travelling bag from the coach. He mounted up then helped Sherin up behind the saddle.

'You'll have to hold the bag on your lap.'

'It's not far to Reeves Hope, I'll be all right.'

Trey was puzzled. 'You seem to know this area pretty good. Are you from these parts?'

Next thing he knew that darned gun was being pressed between the fifth and sixth ribs on his right side.

'That's all your questions used up, Trey. Stop being so curious and get going.'

He laughed again. 'Sure thing, Sherin.' But he wasn't laughing at her, it was the irony of being curious while he was riding on the ridge that had landed him in this weird situation. He'd found the stagecoach, but no silver, only a bundle of mischief.

'Life's full of funny twists and turns,' he said. 'You know, Sherin, I wouldn't even be surprised if we wind up getting married, being husband and wife proper, specially if you stick that little barrel in my ribs to get me to the pastor!' He laughed loudly.

Sherin slipped the gun back into her garter, put her arms round Trey's waist, held on tight and said, 'Dream on, mister.'

Trey pressed his heels lightly into the horse's flanks with a gentle verbal encouragement, anything too violent and Sherin would have fallen off the back and taken him with her. Hoss complained about the extra burden, he never contracted for passengers, but soon moved into a gentle trot and within moments Reeves Hope came into view.

Scanning the street boards for a hotel, Trey had to ride almost to the other end of town before he eyeballed the one and only accommodation. Riding in from the other end it would be the first building that was seen; this way he'd nearly run out of town before finding somewhere to stop. He hitched outside. Sherin slid off the back of the horse with a little help and straightened herself out. She grabbed at Trey and slipped her arm through his. They went up the steps onto the boardwalk.

She said, 'We'll be mister and misses Cormac, that all right with you?'

Trey just tilted his head and chuckled inwardly. It was a preposterous situation and he couldn't help but see the funny side of it.

'Whatever you say, ma'am.'

As he signed the register, the hotel owner's wife, a slightly straight-laced woman with pinched-in cheeks and a sour turn of mouth, gave him a disdainful look and turned her nose up at Sherin. She showed them upstairs to a poky room. By the way she had looked at them, Trey was sure she guessed they weren't husband and wife.

'Too small,' Sherin said without going in. 'You got something better than this?'

The woman closed the door and went along the

19

corridor to another room.

'The biggest we got,' she said, giving Sherin the key and walking away. As she got to the top of the stairs she turned before going down. 'Don't break the bed and no noise after 10 o'clock. That's if you're still here then.'

'Take no notice,' Sherin said, throwing her bag on a chair. 'I need a bath.'

Trey spent the next half hour filling the tub, going up and down the stairs to the kitchen more times than he cared to remember. A screen separated him from the noise and sight of Sherin washing off the dust. Her dress was hanging over the screen, but when she finally emerged she'd changed into a long straight skirt and velvet riding jacket over a white blouse with a flounced ruff. Quite the demure, dutiful wife.

'Well now, I wonder what other outfits you've got in that little carpet bag. Quite a transformation.'

'We'd best get along to the sheriff.'

'I'm sure somebody else will have seen the coach and told him.'

'Even so, I want to tell him myself, after all I was there when it happened.'

Sheriff Anderson's office was back along Main Street. The stagecoach was already outside, being observed by a crowd of people, several offering opinions as to what had happened. Sherin went straight up to the man with the star.

'Sheriff, may I have a word with you inside your office. I was travelling on this coach and can tell you what happened.'

She didn't wait for an answer, she opened the door and walked in, expecting him to follow. The small crowd fell silent watching her give the orders. The sheriff shrugged and followed her up the steps and into the office. He shut the door, Trey was left outside with the crowd. An old geezer with white hair and a wrinkled face waved the crowd back. He was wearing a star, too. A deputy in a town this size? Surely just an unpaid pastime for some old war hero.

Trey peered through the window with the others. Sherin had sat herself in the sheriff's chair and he was standing awkwardly nearby. She was talking and gesticulating, making a gun shape with her hand and probably elaborating. Then she pointed at Trey through the window. The door opened and the sheriff called him in.

'You Trey Cormac?'

'Yes sir, that's me.'

'You know this lady?'

'You mean my . . .' He didn't know what to say and looked at Sherin. She indicated her left-hand ring finger and shook her head.

'You mean this lady?' he said lamely.

'That's what I asked. Step inside.'

'I was riding along the ridge, when I heard shots. . . .' He told the rest of the story exactly how it happened.

Sheriff Anderson turned back to Sherin. 'Now, ma'am. You say there was a strongbox on the coach, full of silver.'

'I don't know for sure what was in the box, but they

21

certainly took it. It was the only thing they were after.'

'And no other passengers?'

'Like I said before, the coach wasn't meant for passengers, I was in a hurry to leave Corburg and I persuaded them to take me along.'

Sherin put her foot up on the desk and revealed a pretty ankle to help the sheriff understand her powers of persuasion. The sheriff turned away, flustered, he poured himself a cup of coffee from the can on the stove. He didn't offer any to anyone else. He put the cup to his lips deep in thought.

'Dang! That's mighty hot.' He put the cup on the desk. 'Well, I guess that's all you can say for now. You staying local?'

'Just down the road,' Trey confirmed.

'If I've got any more questions I'll come looking. Don't leave unless I say so.'

Sherin got up and the sheriff immediately sat in his vacated chair in case anyone else should come in and usurp his position.

They left the office and walked down the street.

As they passed the saloon, Sherin poked Trey in the ribs. 'Say you buy me a drink, Trey.'

'I didn't even have any breakfast yet.'

It wasn't a suggestion, it was a politely given order as she steered him in through the batwings. It was early afternoon and dirty plates were still sitting on some tables from lunchtime service. A lingering smell of stew was unavoidable. There was a low cloud of smoke hanging in its usual place, and a game of cards was being played in a dark corner.

Trey asked if there was any stew, he ordered a beer for himself and a whiskey for Sherin. They sat down, taking off their hats. Sherin shook her head and fluffed up her shining locks. She looked very beautiful as shafts of sunlight highlighted the coppery streaks in her hair. He face was serene and there was the faintest of smiles on her full red lips. She threw her head back and the whiskey disappeared in one gulp. She pushed the glass across to Trey, he signalled to the barman, the bottle was brought across and put on the table.

'I don't think you like me too much, do you Trey? You seem a little uncomfortable.'

It's true he wasn't entirely relaxed, but if he'd been asked he couldn't have said exactly why. There was just the feeling that somehow he wasn't really in control of this situation. He took up his glass and downed a swig of beer. After all, what was he doing in this bar in Reeves Hope drinking with a lady, in the middle of the afternoon? A very attractive lady, but one who seemed to radiate a certain reputation. How had he come across a stagecoach robbery but not immediately followed it up and given chase? With a quick decision he could, more than likely, have caught up with the bandits by riding the ridge until it dropped down into Reeves Hope. Instead he'd ridden down the dangerous scarp to help a lady in distress – this young woman who was now sitting opposite him, drinking whiskey and smiling at him in a self-satisfied manner. He'd certainly given up the chance of a good bounty. This was not like him at all. He was entirely taken up with this copper-haired siren.

It didn't bode well, and what was going to happen when they were back in the hotel room for the night? He'd already decided he would stay on watch and sleep in the chair. On watch for what? Was it simply avoidance?

Just then one of the card players approached their table a little the worse for drink and waving a silver dollar. He was smiling at Sherin.

'Say, lady, this is my last dollar.' He bit it unnecessarily to indicate it was real silver and almost fell into the chair beside Sherin. He laid his arm on the table to steady himself. Trey watched to see how it would play out.

'My last dollar,' he repeated, 'and I'd like to spend it on you!'

Sherin laughed and turned her head away to avoid the fumes. 'One dollar? What do you think you could have for that?'

'Anything I want!'

It was time for Trey to intervene, he stood up and took the fellow by the elbow lifting him gently out of the chair. The man swung round, his hand in the shape of a fist, but a pretty useless one in his state. He punched the air.

'Come on fella,' Trey encouraged. 'A bit of fresh air is what you need, and it won't even cost you a dollar.'

The man was by now almost cross-eyed and staggering. If it wasn't for Trey's support he'd be a jelly on the floor. Stupidly he spoke again.

'Does she cost you more 'an a dollar a time?'

'That's enough of that kinda talk, just mind your mouth.'

24

'I'll bet she's worth it!'

With the back of his hand, Trey slapped the man's face as a warning. 'Ain't no call for that.' He pushed him out through the batwings and the man could be heard falling into the dust and cussing.

Before Trey had sat down the man was pushing his way back in and fumbling around his holster. Amazingly, he managed to pull his six-gun free but before he could do anything with it, Trey took two huge strides across the saloon, wrenched the gun out of the drunk's hand and laid him out with a swift upper cut.

'Bravo!' Sherin said.

'He'll be all right when he's slept it off.'

The barkeep came across, took hold of the man's boots and dragged him over to his friends at the card table. 'Take him home to bed. I don't want to see him again for a week. Got it?'

At a quarter to eleven, in total darkness Trey and Sherin climbed the stairs very quietly so as not to disturb anyone. The treads creaked horribly but nobody stirred. In their room, Sherin plumped down on the bed and tested the springs, bouncing up and down.

'Sssh,' Trey said urgently.

'Aw, come on Trey, you've got to have a bit of fun.'

Trey lit a couple of candles, but as soon as they were alight, Sherin jumped up and pinched them out.

'More fun in the dark,' she said.

'I'm sleeping in the chair,' Trey replied.

*

But in the morning, there's always a price to pay and, waking early, Trey had a sudden and salutary shock.

He sat up in bed and scanned the room. Pale daylight was filtering through the flimsy curtains. Something felt wrong, everything was suspiciously quiet. He stretched out for his pocket watch. It was half past seven. For a moment he tried to recollect what he was doing in this hotel. Had he just stopped for the night? Was he on someone's trail? That was the usual thing, waking up in a flea-ridden bed in some two-bit town, hot on the trail of a bounty. He stroked his chin, hoping it might help him remember. Something wasn't right, but he didn't yet know what. He yawned and slid back down under the covers.

Suddenly it all came back to him, Denver and the silver bars. The stagecoach and the robbery. Oh yes, and that woman. He emerged double quick and felt for his gun-belt hanging on the bed post by his head. He'd half expected it to be gone, but it was still there with the gun. Slowly came the realisation that something had gone; not something, someone, Sherin.

He ran his fingers through his tousled hair and breathed out a sigh of exasperation. Sherin had gone all right, her clothes were gone, her carpet bag was gone, and he never heard her go. Losing his grip. And why was he in the bed? He'd settled down to sleep in the chair. Had she slipped something into his beer? He cursed his stupidity. What a dupe!

He leapt out of bed, shocked to find that he had no clothes on, and went straight for his saddle-bags. He dropped them to the floor in frustration. Sherin and her things was not all that was missing. His wad of bounty money had gone with her, near a thousand hard-earned dollars.

'Damn and blast the woman! Trey Cormac, what a sucker you've been. Taken in by a chorus girl, even if she was a right pretty one, and I never heard her sing!'

He dressed slowly, resigned to a state of penury until the next bounty came in. He probably didn't even have enough spare cash to pay for the hotel room and that would be awkward. He scrabbled around in all the places he hid spare coins and found a little less than two dollars. It might just be enough. He didn't dare ask for hot water to shave, in case it increased the bill. A cold water shave would have to do. Even when he camped out the night, he always had hot water for a shave and some coffee. This was a bad start to the day and it was about to get a lot worse.

3

It was mid-morning when Trey finally decided to go and see Sheriff Anderson. He'd had breakfast at the hotel and avoided paying the bill for the moment, saying he had urgent business with the sheriff and he'd square with them later. The expression on the woman's face need hardly be described, but she let him go without settling up, after all, his horse was still in the yard as collateral.

The sheriff wasn't in his office, but the wizened, old Deputy Bremston offered Trey some coffee while he waited. He accepted and sat down. It wasn't long before the door opened and Anderson came in. He looked surprised.

'Say, sonny. I've just been looking fer you.'

'Me?'

'Yes, you. Got anything you want to tell me?'

Trey was puzzled. 'Yes, I have.'

'That's good,' Anderson said, sitting himself at his desk with his elbows on the edge and his fingertips together. 'Start at the beginning.'

'Beginning? That woman I came in here with, the one I rescued from the hold-up, Sherin, well, I . . . er . . . we . . . er. Let me put it like this . . . er . . . she wanted me to act like her husband. . . .'

Anderson and his deputy looked at one another and raised their eyebrows.

Trey noticed, but ignored it. '. . . she told me she left Corburg in a hurry and I guess wanted to arrive here looking respectable or just like an ordinary married couple or something like that. I don't rightly know. Anyhow, she survived the hold-up and now she's robbed me, taken my wad of a thousand dollars, and ridden off.'

'Ah, I see,' Anderson said with a broad smile. 'She took more payment than you were expecting.'

'I wasn't expecting anything!'

'How old are you, sonny?'

'Twenty-five.'

The deputy laughed. 'Old enough to know better.'

Trey tried to make himself look more important than that. 'Now look fellas, it's not like that. I did her a good turn and she's done the dirty on me. Anyway I'm out of cash now. Look, I'm on official business, I'm on my way to Denver to investigate the manufacture of fake silver ingots. Right now I need to pay the hotel bill, so I need to earn a bit of cash quickly. Can you lend me a couple of dollars, or have you got any reward dodgers I could follow up quickly?'

Anderson opened his desk drawer and pulled out a sheaf of dodgers.

Trey looked through them. He pulled one out. 'Ha!

Slim Coochee, I know that drifter. Been after him for a while.' He pulled out another one. 'Those eyes, kinda wrong shape for a man, or he's a mighty pretty boy called Gonzalez. Just that, nothing more. Looks a bit Mexican with a moustache like that.'

Having indulged Trey for a moment, the sheriff laughed. 'Well, Mr Cormac, I like your style, I really do. You're a smart guy. A bounty hunter working both sides of the law.'

Trey went on fingering through the dodgers. It suddenly clicked what Anderson had said.

'What d'you mean, both sides?'

Bremston fired a quick question. 'Now why d'you leave the stage outside the town?'

'How do you know that?'

Anderson tilted his head. 'It'd be better for you if you told me the whole thing right from the start.'

'I don't understand what you're driving at.'

'Driving? That's good! Do you deny you were driving the stage?'

Trey shrugged. 'I guess not. After I frightened off the bunch of bandits I rode down to the woman to see if she'd been shot. She was all right, just shook up. We picked up the bodies of the driver and guard and brought the stage to town. Just before we got here Sherin said to leave the coach and come in by horse.'

'And why did she do that?'

'You'll have to ask her. She stuck a gun in my ribs.'

The sheriff and deputy looked at each other. A young woman outwitting a seasoned bounty hunter, not very likely.

30

Deputy Bremston probed again. 'Is it because you'd actually been the one who held up the stage. Aren't you the woman's accomplice? That lady got on a bullion stage by subterfuge, fooling the company back in Corburg and planning with you to hold it up just outside here. You already knew Sherin Crew, didn't you? You're a slippery one, Cormac.'

Trey was silent for a moment. He looked from the sheriff to the deputy and back again, his brow furrowed, his expression disbelieving. He stuttered.

'Look, I've been skinned of a thousand dollars and all you're trying to do is fit me up as a stagecoach robber. I'm a bounty hunter, not a ridge rider. I never saw this woman before yesterday, I swear it, and rather wish I hadn't ridden down to save her. Look, I shot one of the robbers in the arm.'

'In that case you wouldn't mind if we search your room.'

'What? In the hotel? Be my guest, you won't find anything interesting. Like I said, she disappeared in the night.'

The morning that had started badly was taking a turn for the worse. Not only had Trey lost a thousand dollars, or thereabouts, and been made to look like a greenhorn, he was now being accused of involvement in the stage robbery. Come to think of it, he didn't even know if the stage had really been robbed. It was Sherin who said there'd been a strongbox on board. Now why had she robbed him and made off, surely she'd realize he'd track her to the ends of the earth and give her a good beating, which is what she deserved, except he wouldn't hit a woman. This was no way to repay a good deed.

By the time he'd thought all that, they were back at the hotel.

The sheriff hit the bell and the woman appeared almost at once.

'Good day, Martha, which room did this young man stay in last night?'

'It hasn't been cleaned yet,' she said. 'And he wasn't alone. A woman. They made a lot of noise. All night.'

'Mind if we go up?'

Martha took the key off the hook. 'And he hasn't paid yet.'

She led the way up the stairs, unlocked the door and pushed it open while stepping back.

The bed was a mess.

'Good night, was it?' Anderson remarked with a smirk. 'Lift the mattress, Bremston.'

The deputy gave it a mighty shove, well beyond his visible strength, pushing it over the bed and dropping the edge to the floor.

The room was silent.

Martha was curious and peered round the door. They were all staring at a small bank sack, stencilled in black $500. Needless to say the seal had been cut off and the bag was empty. Anderson picked it up and looked inside. He pulled out a piece of paper and read it.

'Neat,' Anderson noted. 'Neat. She's left us a note saying it was all your idea and she wants no part of it.'

'But . . .' Trey began.

'Save your breath, sonny. You're under arrest.

32

Bremston take his gun.'

'Now, wait a minute. This is insane. If I knew this was here why didn't I just pack up and ship out? Why would I come and complain about being robbed if I had all this money from these bags, and knew about the note? It doesn't make sense.'

'It sure don't. You'll have plenty of time to figure it out while I decide what to do. Circuit judge isn't due for three weeks, so you've got time to think of a story.'

'I don't need a story, Sheriff, I didn't do it.'

'Yeah, well, we'll see.'

Without his sidearm, being marched back up Main Street to the sheriff's office with the prospect of three weeks in a poky cell, it wasn't surprising Trey was feeling a bit gloomy. There was no point in saying anything. He needed to think this through. Somewhere there'd be an explanation. He only hoped it would arrive before the circuit judge. Stagecoach robbery usually ended in hanging.

At least there was a rough blanket in the one and only cell, and a wooden bed made up of two planks joined and attached to the wall with chains. A table was furnished with a tin mug and a jug of water.

'Is the grub any good?' Trey asked hopefully as the heavy iron gate was closed and locked.

Deputy Bremston responded with a toothless laugh. 'What grub?'

'Will someone get my horse into livery?'

Bremston smiled. 'Don't worry son, we've got all your gear. It'll be divided up when the judge has finished with you.'

33

Trey wasn't sure if it was a joke. Either way it was in bad taste. He let the bed down on its chains, it was somewhere to sit.

'Hey, Anderson, any chance of some coffee?'

There was no reply and he couldn't even see if the sheriff was sitting at his desk.

'Say, sheriff, got a book I could read?'

This got a response. Anderson came round the corner with a book in his hand. He turned it sideways and held it through the vertical bars. Trey took it with a thank you. He sat on the planks. The front cover sported a big gold cross.

Anderson's dismembered voice bounced off the wall at him.

'Heard of the book of Deuteronomy?'

'Not sure, I guess so.'

'Try chapter twenty-four, verse seven.'

Trey opened the sheriff's Bible and flicked through the Old Testament to the fifth book and thumbed down the pages until he came to verse seven in the twenty-fourth chapter. He read out loud.

If a man be found stealing any of his brethren of the children of Israel, and maketh merchandise of him, or selleth him; then that thief shall die; and thou shall put evil away from among you.

'I ain't stole no person,' Trey called out.

The answer came from round the corner. 'Person, money, goods. All the same thing in the eyes of the law, Cormac. Evil has to be put away from amongst us! S'pose you tell me where the money is?'

'Were you ever a minister?'

34

Anderson laughed. 'Did the woman take it? Your accomplice. I suggest you carry on reading, son. There's still time to repent.'

Trey wasn't sure whether the sheriff was serious or just joshing with him; at least he had something to pass the time of day. His Bible-reading days were way back in the past. His folks had been good Christian God-fearing people and he'd had a good enough education in Sunday school, good enough to be able to read and do sums, that's all he really needed. His pa had taught him how to shoot and his ma had taught him the fundamentals of cooking. As a free-ranging bounty hunter that's about all he needed. He could shoot the bandits, cook up some grub, read the reward dodgers and count out the bounty. What more did he need? Life had treated him well.

But now, ignominiously, he'd been completely taken in and double-crossed by a pretty young woman. What might have been promising had certainly taken a turn for the worse.

He opened the book at the first chapter, Genesis, how the world began. He flicked through to the next heading, Exodus. He vaguely remembered Exodus was full of good stories and above all it was about escape. Maybe he'd get some ideas. But why? Why had Sherin done this? Was it really for his thousand dollars?

He put the book down and tried to think. What possible motive could Sherin have for framing him, what did she gain from it?

'Hey, Anderson, I don't suppose you'd let me out

35

on bail, so I could go and catch this woman?'

'You're right, I wouldn't. You can't put up bail.'

Trey smiled to himself. 'I've got a couple of silver dollars says I could go and look for her.'

'Get back to your reading. And hush up, I don't want to listen to you whining for the next three weeks.'

Three weeks is a mighty long time when you've got nothing to do and only the Bible to read. Trey was thankful for the loan of the book, but his days were an endless round of boredom. To be fair to Anderson, he shackled Trey and let Bremston walk him round the back yard for a half hour every day. The fresh air was good and the sunshine warmed him through, but he couldn't help trying to devise a scheme to make his escape. However, nothing had any real chance of succeeding.

He ploughed through Exodus and then moved on to the New Testament. He remembered enough of the Sunday school stories to know that Jesus had faced trial and humiliation with an equanimity and resignation that shone above everything else, yet, like Jesus, he too was innocent. The biggest shock had been when Anderson casually announced that the robbery was a minor charge. There was also the matter of the shooting to death of the driver and guard.

As the visit of the circuit judge came ever nearer Trey began to think very hard about how he was going to convince a jury of twelve local men, honest or not, that he had nothing to do with the robbery, let alone the murder of the two stagecoach employees. Anderson and Bremston hadn't given up on cajoling him to confess. They'd tried to trick him by saying they'd put in a good word with the jury if he admitted it was all planned. In any case, they had the note from Sherin, which more or less convicted him; his only hope of leniency was confession.

He must have been well and truly doped up on some locoweed concoction not to have woken up during the night. But why frame him? The obvious reason was that it exonerated her. But it still didn't feel right.

The next day Anderson came round the corner from his office. There was another gentleman with him, a tall guy with a grey frock coat, white shirt, black bootlace tie and waistcoat. He was smoking a cigar.

'Someone to see you, Cormac. This is Judge Junison.' Anderson turned to the judge. 'This is Trey Cormac, robber, thief, murderer. Been here three weeks, no confession.'

Trey leapt to his feet. 'Innocent man, Judge, I never did anything to that stage nor those two men. I did nothing but assist a lady in distress. Now she's framed me up.'

The judge smiled at him and spoke to Anderson. 'He's right, Anderson. Innocent, innocent until proved guilty. But I guess that won't take the jury too long.'

'Hey, wait a minute. . . .'

'No, you wait a minute, Mr Cormac,' the judge began, rather severely. 'Evil has to be rooted out. We want a peaceful community in this part of the state. Law-abiding citizens must be free to go about their business without fear of being robbed or murdered.'

Trey opened his hands in an expansive gesture. 'Judge, I'm a bounty hunter. I've brought dozens to justice. . . .'

'And so you must face the music when you transgress. Past deeds are of no use when good men turn bad.' The judge pointed to the Bible on the table. 'I see you have a copy of the good book. Make your peace with the Lord, Mr Cormac.'

They both turned away and left Trey clutching the bars. Was his life really going to end like this?

That night Trey slept hardly a wink. Although he couldn't see out to the street, moonlight painted one of the windows on the wooden floorboards in front of his cell. As the night slowly moved towards day the image of the window moved across the floor contrary-wise to the passage of the moon across the sky. He wanted it to hurry up so he could plead his case before the forbidding figure of Judge Junison and explain exactly what happened on that unlucky day, hoping that justice would prevail.

With the thought of a bad outcome from the twelve jurymen of Reeves Hope, Trey ruminated on the worst part of his dilemma. The one thing that irked him more than anything else was Sherin's wicked betrayal. He still couldn't fathom what had driven her to do it, and why she had left all the evidence that would put him squarely in the frame. Was she really that kind of low-life?

He wished he could remember more of the night in question. How could he give the judge a convincing story if he really didn't have a clue what had happened? Hell, he was going to look pretty silly in court having to explain how he'd been fooled by a pretty young woman, especially as she looked the kind who'd be pleased to earn a couple of dollars and had actually run away with fifteen hundred. He could just imagine the courtroom filling with raucous laughter. But at the same time, he refused to believe Sherin was that kind of girl. Yes, she had the looks of a real saloon beauty, and knew how to use her charm, but something still didn't add up.

Puzzling that conundrum, Trey fell into the deepest sleep of the night. The next thing he heard was the cell door being unlocked and Bremston clanking a tray on the little table. Anderson was standing outside the cell, gun drawn.

4

Bremston gave Trey a shove. 'Wake up, Cormac, Martha in the hotel has sent up a breakfast for you, there's hot coffee, too. You're going need your wits about you today.'

He left the cell, pulling the door with a loud clang. Trey swung himself off the plank bed and sat up. Stubble itched his chin, he scratched and pondered on Martha's generosity. A sour face doesn't mean a mean spirit.

'Hey, Anderson, can I have a shave? I need to look smart for the judge.'

A half hour later, breakfast finished, an elderly barber arrived with a bowl of hot water, soap, a towel and a razor. Bremston stood outside the cell, gun drawn. The barber stood in front of Trey, set the things down, put the towel round Trey's neck, then flashed open the razor with an unpleasant smile and a glint in his eye.

'Just give me the word, son, and I'll save you the bother of the trial.'

Trey pulled the towel off his neck. 'I've changed my mind. Get this man out of my cell!'

At half past ten, Anderson got up from his desk, took some handcuffs off a peg and went around the corner to open the cell door.

Trey looked up. 'Is it time?'

'Your moment has arrived. Court's all ready and you're the first case today.'

Trey was cuffed. Bremston took him by the arm, Anderson went out first and walked in front of them across the street to the courthouse. It was just a saloon, of course. Reeves Hope was too small to have a court-house, it was too small to be on the judge's circuit, but Anderson must have sent a request saying his prisoner was too dangerous to move him around the county.

The tables had been removed, chairs set out in a couple of rows. A more impressive chair had been found for the judge and the jurors had to make do with two long benches. The room was already full of local people, it seemed overcrowded and stuffy. Bremston pushed Trey to the front and sat him down on a chair at the side. Anderson stood at the front to address the crowd.

'Now folks, don't forget this man is innocent until the jury find him guilty. An' just a reminder that if you're wearing a sidearm, kindly leave it at the bar. There's to be no shoutin', screamin', nor nothin' like that. This is an orderly town and I'd like it to stay that way. Bremston, go and get the judge.'

The room settled to a quiet hum of chat. Trey began to feel the sweat on his palms. Somehow up to

41

this point, it hadn't seemed quite real, now the full implication of his predicament was dawning. He scanned the rough, unshaven faces of the twelve jurors. Their sallow complexions, pinched cheeks and dry lips gave him no encouragement. The fact that the jurors weren't even looking at him, but talking to each other, filled him with insignificance, almost of his presence being totally irrelevant. They were all just waiting for the judge to deliver him up for hanging. It was an unjust end.

A moment later everyone was on their feet. Anderson strode down the side of the room in front of Judge Junison and led him to his chair. It was almost theatrical. The judge sat down, everybody sat down. One of the jurors stood up.

'Your honour, we find this man guilty of murder and robbery. . . .'

'Hold on there,' Junison said, raising his hand to curb the juror's enthusiasm. 'It's not your turn yet. The sheriff has to speak first. Let's get it in the right order. This court is now in session. Anderson, say your piece.'

What followed was almost incomprehensible to Trey. It was the most damning list of lies he'd ever heard. He'd been portrayed as a wanted desperado, out looking for trouble and had ended up killing two innocent men, robbing the stage of a bank consignment of some several thousand dollars, holding a young woman hostage, having his way with her while she was tied to the bed, and falsely accusing her of stealing his money.

On the basis of those lies it was inevitable that the same juror was going to stand up again and repeat the lines that he'd obviously been taught to say the night before.

Junison turned to Trey. 'I guess you won't deny any of those accusations. Don't forget you've sworn on the Bible to tell the truth and these good, God-fearing people deserve to hear the truth. . . .'

At that moment there was a commotion at the door. A man burst through with a six-gun in one hand and a shot-gun in the other. He fired a pistol shot into the roof. Everyone ducked and covered their ears.

'Hold it right there.' The voice was a bit high pitched with adrenalin but the shot-gun was waved side to side across the room and everyone knew what that was capable of at such short range.

'I want the prisoner. Sheriff, take off the cuffs. Nobody move or innocent people will die.'

While he was speaking he walked carefully round the room with his back to the wall. His bandanna was pulled up over his mouth but his eyes darted round the crowd, and from sheriff to deputy in case they tried to draw. Trey was released and told to take the guns from the sheriff and deputy. The man pointed the shot-gun at the judge, while giving Anderson a clear order.

'I'm going to count to fifty slowly. Get down to the hotel and get his horse, all his gear and bring it back here before the judge gets his head blown off.'

The atmosphere in the room had gone from hot to boiling. Nobody dared to speak, the stillness was unnatural. Trey pointed the sheriff's gun at the juror who had spoken out of turn.

'Who taught you your lines?'

The juror turned white. 'Look mister, I don't know nothin' 'bout what you done. I was just told to say that.'

'And you'd have hung an innocent man.' He turned to the crowd. 'I don't know who this man is who's come to rescue me, but he's the only decent one here. My name's Trey Cormac, I'm innocent of all these lying charges and don't you forget it.'

It wasn't long before Anderson came back into the saloon, hands raised. 'Your horse is here.'

Trey and his rescuer backed out of the saloon. The man mounted his horse while Trey kept the door open and the gun trained on the crowd. Then he leapt up into the saddle and the two of them rode off down Main Street at full pelt.

Just before the end of the street Trey shouted out 'Stop!'

They both pulled up. Trey asked the masked man for a few dollars. He fished about in his saddle-bag, a quizzical look in his eyes peering above the bandanna.

Trey dashed into the hotel, slapped the dollars on the counter, rushed back out and mounted up.

The masked man pointed back up the street where people were spilling out of the saloon. He shook his head and they rode off for the hills.

Fearing a posse, but suspecting the poor townsfolk of Reeves Hope lived more by hope than action, Trey and his rescuer didn't bother to ride more than a quarter mile into the wooded cover of the foothills before they stopped. It was time for a few questions.

The man pulled the mask down off his face revealing a ridiculously large bushy moustache. He took the corner and peeled the moustache off with a slight grimace as the glue pulled at his upper lip. And what a lovely upper lip it was.

'Sherin! You . . . you . . . what the hell?'

'So that's all the thanks I get?'

'Thanks? You stitched me up like a mailbag. You could've got me hanged. Should I be grateful for that?'

'For saving you, yes.'

Trey couldn't help himself. He had to laugh. 'I just hope it's a good story, 'cos I can't wait to hear it. What the hell is going on?'

Sherin pressed her heels lightly into her horse and it moved off at a walk. The track was wide enough for them to ride side by side. Trey fell back a little, wondering what might happen next.

Sherin spoke over her shoulder. 'You don't remember anything do you?'

'Of what? The night that I ended up in the bed without a stitch to my name, and then you gone in the morning.' He drew up level. 'You haven't got the slightest notion what a dilemma that gave me. And when did you plant that bank bag and note under the mattress?'

Sherin turned and smiled at him. 'Ha! You really don't remember, do you! The bag was under the bed long before you got in with me.'

45

'I got in with you?'

'Yeah.'

'I don't believe it. I was in the chair.'

Sherin laughed. 'Well the only reason you're here now is because you were a lot of fun.'

'Fun?'

'You know what I mean. You were good. I realized something had been slipped into your drink and that you were going to face the music on your own. That's why I came back for you today.'

'And I'm supposed to believe all that?'

'Well, you're here, aren't you? And so am I.'

Trey heaved out a great sigh. He didn't know what to believe. On the other hand he couldn't refute any of what Sherin had said. But he wasn't finished yet.

'Do you have any idea what it's like to be cooped up in a poky cell all day for three weeks with only the Bible to read?'

'It should make you full of forgiveness and repentance. Anyway, I need you. Don't dwell on the negative side of things.'

'It's kinda hard not to, when I've just come so close to being handed down a death sentence.'

'Now you're being dramatic! You weren't in any danger, not ever. I was your guardian angel.'

Trey had no answer to that for the moment. Sherin decided they'd been dawdling long enough. There was not likely to be any posse, but she spurred on and they started to canter along the rough track and into the hills. Soon they were alternating trotting and cantering to cover as much distance as possible.

'We could stop out here for the night,' Trey suggested. 'You've got a bedroll and I've got all my gear. We can't make the next town before nightfall. I could shoot something for dinner.'

Sherin made no reply, but as the sun started to go down she nodded to Trey and told him to keep his eyes open for a good spot. Within the hour, a camp was made and a fire picking up. Trey had skinned two rabbits, shot cleanly through the head, and he'd rigged up a stick above the fire to roast the meat. When all was ready they sat down to a satisfying bite. They shared a mug of coffee, then another. Trey rolled a smoke, lit it and offered it to Sherin. She took it, had a couple of puffs and passed it back. Now was an opportunity for Trey to find out a bit more about this woman.

'You told me, when I first rescued you at the stage hold-up that you were running away from Corburg and someone or something, and in a bit of a hurry.'

'Well that's true. I was.' She paused. 'In a bit of a hurry.'

'Had you done something wrong? The law chasing you?'

'No.'

'But tell me, why did you have a bank bag from the stage. Didn't the robbers take the strongbox and all the money?'

'Yes they did, but they left one bag behind and I just put it in my luggage for safe keeping.'

Trey snorted. 'Safe keeping? You must have had a reason to keep the bag, especially as it could incriminate you.'

47

'Sometimes you just do things not knowing why at the time, but it comes in useful later.'

'For pinning the blame on someone else, for example.'

Sherin nodded. 'For example, yes.'

Trey shook his head. 'You're a sly one, Sherin Crew, I can't afford to turn my back without wondering what you're thinking. Now tell me why you came back to rescue me from summary justice and the end of a rope. I don't believe it had anything to do with what you said.'

Sherin cocked her head to one side and smiled at Trey. 'You don't believe you were good fun.'

'Hell I don't even know what you're talking about.'

'Well then don't dwell on it. Let's just be glad neither of us came to any harm. Reeves Hope hasn't suffered any loss.'

'But what about those two men, the coach driver and guard? They're both dead.'

'Yes, that was unfortunate.'

Trey took a swig of coffee and passed the cup to Sherin. He didn't like the way she had just glibly dismissed the murder of two stagecoach employees. Men maybe with a family that would now be without a wage, young kids perhaps.

Sherin seemed to guess what Trey was thinking. 'Sometimes people die for no good reason, sometimes they get in the way, sometimes they're infantry in the line of fire. It wasn't my fault.'

'That's no way for a woman to talk.'

Sherin shook her head. 'Look, it's only a few years

since the Yanks faced down Johnny Reb. Bad people died, good people died, too. Sometimes good people have to die when there are bigger things going on. A more important end in sight.'

'If I didn't know you were a woman I'd have thought you fought in the war.'

'Well, I am a woman and I didn't,' she replied somewhat offended.

Trey narrowed his eyes. 'There's something goin' on you're not telling me. I don't trust all this nonsense about good people dying, about the murder of those two men, about getting me locked up. And what's happened to the shipment of silver bars? I need to find them. What are you up to?'

Sherin shifted her position nearer to Trey, she was almost leaning on him, her head very close to his shoulder. It made him both excited and cautious at the same time. He was beginning to realize his experience with women was not very great. Casual encounters in cow towns was about the long and short of it, so he was susceptible to the appeal of a woman sitting quite close. The heat from the fire was not all that was warming his blood.

'You said trust,' Sherin began, 'that's the word you used and that's at the heart of it. Who can I trust?'

'Is that a question? Are you expecting an answer?'

She continued. 'No, it's not a question really, it's just a thought.'

'Ah, I see your game. You stitch me up, then rescue me to test me, to see if you can trust me, see if I squeal like a pig or stay quiet like a mule. You can trust a

49

mule to do the job, but you can't a trust a pig to do nothing. Is that it? What do you want me to do? Hunt someone down?'

Sherin yawned. 'It's been a long day.'

She got up and rolled out her bed a few steps away from Trey, placing her saddle at the head for a pillow. 'You'd better put some more wood on the fire. I'll see you in the morning.'

'Guess so,' Trey replied, but he wasn't in a hurry to sleep.

He placed some more logs on the fire and sat watching the flames and listening to the crackling of the branches turning to charcoal. He glanced at Sherin's form lit up by the fire. She was lying on her side, turned away from the flames, motionless, maybe asleep already. If trust was the question, she must be very trusting of him having turned her back and gone to sleep. Like it or not he was feeling very protective of this young woman, but there was still something that just didn't add up. He puzzled so hard that he fell asleep sitting upright resting against his saddle and not even in his bedroll.

Whatever she was about, Sherin had cast some deep and troubling spell over his mind. When the moon was three-quarters of its way across the heavens, he woke with a sudden start and instinctively pulled his gun.

50

5

Trey was stone cold. He wasn't dead, just chilled to the core. He had no idea what had disturbed him, maybe the bark of a grey fox or a coyote, but more than likely the cold had at last penetrated right through to his bones. He leant across to the small woodpile and laid some greasewood on the smouldering heap of shimmering charcoal and hot ash. Sherin stirred but didn't wake. He slipped his boots off and slid into the bedroll that was waiting beside him, unused. He shivered, immediately felt warmer and in a moment drifted back into the land of oblivion.

It was Sherin who woke him, not gently, but with the toe of her boot.

'Well, mister, I could have robbed you all over again! Only this time I've taken pity on you and made you some coffee. You must have built a good fire last night, it was still burning this morning.'

Trey was on the point of saying something but decided against it. He sat up and took the mug, muttering a word of thanks.

Sherin took some biscuit and dried beef out of her saddle-bag. 'Here,' she said, handing it to Trey. This'll keep you going until we get to Copps Creek. We'll be there early afternoon. You need a shave.'

Trey felt the stubble. 'Well I nearly got one yesterday morning before they took me off to the courthouse, but didn't fancy the look of the barber. It can wait.'

'You're starting to look like an outlaw,' she mused, looking sideways at him. 'You know, it actually makes you look quite handsome. Forget the shave.'

Trey eased himself out of his bedroll and got into his boots. He was still chewing on the beef. Sherin had loaded her kit and was checking the cinch before she mounted up. Trey kicked out the fire and as he climbed into his saddle he wondered what game Sherin was now playing. She had just said he looked handsome, this was a new angle. While he was well aware that Sherin was a very pretty young woman, he wouldn't share his thoughts with her in case she thought he was taking a shine to her. Why was she flattering him again? Trey's guard went up, she was trying to play with his emotions and he was deeply suspicious of her motives.

Sherin went in front and they soon picked up a rough track through the brushwood and needle grass. She didn't seem to be in too much of a hurry and they ambled along through the open country at something between a fast walk and a slow trot. The track eventually widened and Trey drew up alongside.

'How come you know these tracks so well?'

52

'I don't really, just following instinct.'

Trey sensed that wasn't true. Nobody would have this knowledge, unless they'd ridden these tracks before. Even using the sun for direction, anyone'd have to know roughly where he was. If Trey had been on his own headed for Denver he'd have followed the road used by the stagecoach. This was well off that beaten track. He needed to probe.

'So, tell me what you were doing in Corburg and how you came to be leaving it in such a hurry. You were lucky they gave you a ride on that coach.'

'Lucky! I was nearly killed in the hold-up. I might have been if you hadn't saved me. Or maybe worse.'

'Were you running out on a man?'

'Kinda. But not what you're thinking.'

'Sherin, I ain't thinkin' nothin', just asking. Don't say if you don't want to.'

She looked at him and shrugged. 'Not much to tell really. I thought it was love, but eventually I realized I was being used. It's what happens to girls out west, it takes an age to find a man who you think'll treat you right. He does for a while, then sweet grapes turn to vinegar and you have to choose between a life of bitterness or run away.'

'And that's what you chose.'

'What sort of a choice do you think it is?'

Sympathetically Trey turned towards her, but she didn't look at him, just stared ahead and bit her lip.

The pace quickened and they rode on in silence for a good half hour, Sherin leading the way. At the foot of a gentle incline they slowed to a trot to rest the

53

horses. Trey took the opportunity to ride alongside where the track allowed.

Sherin said, 'What about you?'

'Not much to tell about that either. I grew up on a farm. My folks had a bad time in the war and lost almost everything while I was away fighting . . .'

Sherin jumped in. 'What colour was your uniform.'

'Dark at night, grey when covered in dust, no colour at all at other times.'

'That's a smart answer. Which generals did you fight for?'

Trey smiled, he wasn't going to be caught out like that. 'I fought for freedom. Freedom to do as you please, what you like when you like. I survived, that's all that mattered.'

'And now?'

'And now I hunt. Mostly robbers, murderers, ridge riders, low scum, the trash that think they can just take what others have worked hard to build.'

'Because of your parents?'

'Maybe. My pa was shot in the leg because he refused to give up the hogs as provisions. They took them anyway. I would have been a farmer I guess but there was nothing left at the end of the war. They grew vegetables and kept a few chickens and hoped life would treat them fair until they passed. It didn't.'

'There's bitterness in your voice, Trey.'

'Maybe we get on good, you and me, because we both know what it is to lose.'

Sherin pressed, she knew there was more. 'Then what else have you lost? A girl?'

'It wasn't anything. Just good friends.'

'But you wanted more?'

'Not really. I'm fine like I am. What you haven't got can't be taken away.'

Sherin guessed that wasn't the whole story but she didn't want to open old wounds.

In another few minutes they reached the top of the ridge. Copps Creek could now be seen down in the valley a couple of hours' ride. Trey let Sherin lead the way down a short steep track. He admired her horse-manship; she was no ordinary woman, she'd learnt to ride and could handle a horse with consummate ease. He was impressed. Then he remembered she'd mas-queraded as a man brandishing a six-gun when she took him out of the saloon courtroom at Reeves Hope. She was still carrying the sidearm. Trey wondered if she was also a good shot as well as a good rider. It raised questions in his mind that he wanted to ask, but decided against it. There was a more pressing matter needing an answer.

'Are you stopping at Copps Creek, Sherin?'

'Of course,' she replied, furrowing her brow. 'Did you think I saved you, for you to go riding off on your own?'

'Hadn't given it much thought.'

'Well Trey Cormac, you'd better, because we're still mister and misses Cormac. I haven't yet said you're free to go on your way.'

Trey laughed out loud. 'That's good. Real good. You think you could stop me?'

'No.'

55

'Then . . ?'

'I have friends who will find you.'

'Really? This is getting better by the minute.'

'Trey, there is something you have to know. My friends are dangerous, while you're with me you're safe. The minute we separate, your life is in danger.'

'Oh yes, and I suppose they've been watching our every move. Don't tell me, they're tracking us even now.'

Sherin didn't bother to stop or to look at Trey. 'You must believe whatever you want, but it would be better if we check into the Golden Horse together.'

'The Golden Horse?'

She shouted over her shoulder. 'The hotel in Copps Creek.'

'So you have been here before.' But it was lost on the wind as he spurred his horse to keep up with Sherin.

Sherin didn't look back, she'd quickened the pace now they were down off the ridge and Trey had to gallop for a while to catch up.

It was late afternoon when they hitched outside the Silver Horse hotel. Trey noticed the discrepancy in the name but didn't say anything. The fact that Sherin knew even part of the name was suspicious enough. Although Sherin was still dressed looking very manly with her trousers, jacket, gun-belt and riding boots, when she took her hat off and shook her hair out to fall in a copper cascade over her shoulders, she was every inch a woman. Trey opened the hotel door and Sherin went in. She took Trey's arm as they approached the desk. Trey hit the bell.

Their room was large and bright. It was well furnished and there were windows on two sides. For a small town, this was a comfortable hotel. Sherin had asked for hot water when they checked in and there was soon a knock on the door. A young lad made several trips to fill the bath tub. When he was done, Sherin suggested Trey take a walk while she soaked in the tub.

'Perhaps I'll get a shave,' Trey suggested.

'No, keep the stubble, I like it.'

'Then maybe I'll stay here.'

Sherin picked up the bar of soap and threw it at him. 'Get out,' she said, half serious.

Trey ducked, retrieved the soap and tossed it into the tub before closing the door behind him. He jumped down the stairs, went through into the saloon and ordered a beer. He sat at a table and, staring at the golden liquid in the glass, started to reflect on recent events. He was on his way to Denver to make some enquiries, but first off to find a stagecoach with the silver bars. On route, quite unexpectedly, he had come across the stage being held up just outside Reeves Hope. What had followed since then was almost incomprehensible. A ridiculous situation with an equally ridiculous accusation, three weeks in jail, a surprise rescue and now he was shackled with this young woman. Yes, she was a real stunner, but, somewhat shamefaced, he'd been drugged and spent the night with her, so she claims, while acting like husband and wife. And what for? Where was all this leading? The only reason he was still with her was because they were apparently both going in the same direction. He had dismissed the idea that he was in danger if he left her. Rather to the contrary, he was feeling kind of protective. The silly talk about her friends tracking him down weighed not even a couple of ounces on his conscience, that was just talk. So why didn't he just get up, get his horse out of livery, and clear out?

Being wise after the event is something that almost everyone can be expert in, including Trey Cormac. Seeing what is coming requires a special kind of cleverness and most people, including Trey Cormac, are much less clever at that. Had he been gifted with that kind of knowledge, he wouldn't even have finished his drink, he'd have left in such a hurry he'd probably have forgotten to pay the barkeep. But, an hour after sitting down, he was still there, and deciding that Sherin must have finished her bath, it would be all right to return to the room.

He knocked on the door before going in, waiting for Sherin to say yes, and entered when she did. She was sitting at the dressing table combing her hair. She was wearing her fancy long dress and looked good in it. She had put something black on her eyes and looked even more lovely than he remembered.

She looked up at Trey, her eyes sparkling. 'I thought we'd have a nice quiet dinner together, spend some time chatting or dancing, what d'you say? Some poker perhaps.'

'You play cards?'

'Of course, don't you?'

Trey was mystified, Sherin constantly surprised him. He said, 'I only play when I think it's safe. And just for fun. Too many people end up dead or broke. You wouldn't play in a pokey town like this, would you?'

She shrugged her shoulders and went back to her preening.

The hotel owner recommended another saloon to eat in; his own kitchen was without a cook at the moment and the saloon down the road did good food. It was a short walk away. The saloon was larger than the one attached to the hotel and it was busy. Trey's eyes were immediately drawn to three pokes sitting at a table, they were eyeing him closely in return. There were a couple of card games in progress and a rather scruffy fellow was playing a fiddle accompanied by a piano player. A few lively folk were dancing to the music. Trey and Sherin found a table and sat down. They ordered food and drinks. They chatted. The food arrived, a good beef stew with potatoes and carrots. They drank beer and whiskey, and Sherin drank and ate the same things as Trey. As the evening wore on Sherin suggested they might dance, but she changed her mind and said they should join a game of poker.

'It depends on what rules they're playing,' Trey remarked.

Sherin nodded. 'I've been watching, it seems ordinary enough. A couple of cards each, and five face-up.'

'That can give very good hands. High hands and

high stakes. You sure you want to play?'

Sherin nodded, she saw a player get up and go. She tapped Trey on the knee and slipped him a bundle of paper dollars. He took them, frowning.

'Where in hell . . . are these mine?'

'Hush up,' she said sharply, 'and join that table.'

'Which one?'

She pointed. 'Join them on your own and be careful.'

Trey got up and joined the table with the vacant seat.

'Can I join you, gentlemen?'

They nodded their assent and he sat down, placing a small stack of paper dollars on the table. The four players immediately set their eyes on the money that they hoped to remove from this newcomer, while Trey eyed them all with some suspicion.

'We prefer silver coin,' said one, who introduced himself as Bud. 'This here is Chad, that's Rick and he's Ben. What's your name, stranger?'

Bud was clearly the man in charge. He was middle aged, greying at the temples, a shaggy Civil War moustache under a prominent nose. He was wearing a silk waistcoat with a gold watch chain. Of the other three there was not much to choose between their surly looks. Weasel-like Chad appeared sly with his mean mouth, Rick thin and of a nervous demeanour, Ben's eyes were darting all over the place like a nervous dog.

'The name's Trey, and I don't have coin, only paper.'

Having inspected the paper dollars, Bud passed

Trey the cards. 'Well, let's see how you deal, mister.'

Trey dealt the cards, one each, two up, a round of betting, then one more each and to the middle, then the final two face up in the middle. The five face up showed the three of clubs, the jack of hearts, two, five and queen of diamonds. Nothing spectacular on the table. Trey watched the other players carefully as they turned up their two cards. He pretended to be looking at his, but watched their eyes to see which cards on the table they were looking at, hoping he might get an idea of their hands. Chad opened the betting.

'I'll raise you all.'

The rest followed, nobody folded.

When it came to Trey, he had a queen in his hand, making a pair with the one on the table.

'I'll raise,' he said, placing some dollars on the pile.

'And I'll match it,' said Rick, staring at Trey, but Trey was not intimidated.

The betting continued until the show. Trey's pair of queens did not win. Bud's diamond flush beat everyone.

Another two games proceeded without incident, but Trey began to feel uncomfortable.

On the next deal, Bud's, Trey watched the shuffle closely and saw Bud flip the deck long enough to see the bottom card, an ace, before dealing. Just as Trey suspected, it was a bad deal with the ace clumsily slipped off the bottom of the deck into Bud's own hand. He glanced at Sherin and she shook her head. He realized then that she was watching intently. On this hand Trey was tempted to fold as a pair of threes was never going to win anything. But he stayed in until the pile was high with silver coin and his paper dollars, guessing they were the dollars Sherin had stolen from him. Bud was the winner again with an ace high flush. Cards were thrown in and Bud had his hand on the money.

'Hold it right there, mister.'

The players froze.

6

Sherin stood up and walked over to the table. She put her left hand on Bud's shoulder and smiled sweetly at him. Lowering herself to his level, she gently slipped her arm right across his back as if in an embrace. But at the same time, with her right hand she slowly lifted his six-gun out of its holster.

She stepped back, cocked the gun with a click and the saloon fell silent.

'I'd say you have a little explaining to do about that ace. The one that came off the bottom of the deck.'

Bud stayed cool. 'I don't know what you mean, lady.'

'Take the ace away and what have you got? Just a little biddy pair with the cards on the table. How sad. Now push that money across to Rick. I can see his three of a kind beats you and Chad and Ben and Trey, so pass it over.'

Rick was nervous. 'That's all right with me, lady, Bud won the hand fair and square and I don't want no trouble.'

'You heard the man,' Bud sneered, 'so back off ma'am, and take your poodle with you. I thought you were decent folk, and just being friendly.'

Suddenly Chad leant back in his chair and, without drawing his gun, swivelled the holster and aimed an upwards shot across the table at Sherin. He hadn't leant back far enough and the bullet crashed into the side of the table, sending a shower of splinters into the air. Trey leapt to his feet and smashed his fist into Chad's jaw, sending both him and the chair flying across the floor, crashing into another table where he remained motionless.

People dived for cover under the tables, behind the bar or out of the batwings. The barkeep pulled a shotgun from under the counter. The saloon was filled with drifts of acrid smoke, the reverberation of the gunshot and the sound of tumbling furniture.

Sherin remained motionless, the six-gun pointing at Bud with the firing pin cocked. Rick had sensibly put his hands in the air and fidgeted uncomfortably in his chair. Ben had followed suit. Trey stood by the table, his eyes fixed on Bud and Sherin. For safety he put his hand on his gun, ready to draw. Shortly, three men entered via the batwings, one of whom was sporting a star. Sherin's eyes flicked to the group.

'This man dealt off the bottom of the deck, Sheriff. I'd be obliged if you'd take him into custody so we can all relax.'

The sheriff crossed slowly to the card table, ignoring Sherin. 'Bud? What d'you say?'

'I ain't done nothin', Kyle. But for safety's sake

you'd better get me out of here before this mad bitch loses control.'

With a neat, swift move, Sherin cracked the pistol across the back of Bud's head. He slumped forward, hands limp by his side, jaw resting on the edge of the table, mouth open, tongue lolling and a trickle of blood where he had bitten his cheek.

'Don't you dare call me that, mister. You low-down two-bit tubscum. Get him out of here, Sheriff, and lock him up for the night or I'll pepper him better than a steak.'

The sheriff was clearly not a man of much resolve, probably just seeing out his elected obligation, so Sherin turned to Trey.

'Give the sheriff a hand. Take this turkey to the lock-up and see he turns the key, or I'll not be responsible for what I do.'

The sheriff threw up his hands. 'All right, ma'am, easy up.' He looked round the room, almost pleading for support. 'Did anybody else see Bud deal off the deck?'

Nobody answered.

Trey spoke out. 'He sure did. You best believe it or this will end badly.'

Trey lifted the dazed Bud out of his chair and marched him across to the batwings. 'Sheriff, get his other arm, now let's go.'

The sheriff, wisely, with the help of his two companions, took charge of Bud and walked him out of the saloon. Trey walked behind them, gun drawn, to make sure Bud was given a night in the lock-up.

In the saloon, Sherin was still in charge. 'The show's over, folks. Get this place straightened out and let's all have some fun.'

She eased the firing pin back and scooped up some of the dollars off the table. 'Barkeep, drinks all round on me! Rick, Ben, take what you put into the pot and I'll have the rest.'

'What about Ch . . ?' was as far as Rick got with his silly question before he realized he was being let off lightly. He took some of the coin, stood up and nervously indicated the batwings. Sherin nodded. Ben picked Chad up from the floor, still nursing his jaw, and the three of them left the saloon.

Sherin gave Bud's gun to the barkeep to look after. The barkeep shook his head. 'That wasn't a wise move, ma'am. Bud owns this town and everything in it.'

'Well, he doesn't own me!' she said with a scowl just as Trey came back in smiling.

'Trey, come on. Now we can have that dance. Where's the fiddler gone? Ah there you are, get out of that cupboard and play us a tune.'

And so the evening rolled on in a very light-hearted mood until the sheriff came back in and had a quiet word with Sherin.

'Ma'am, Bud is a big noise in this town, owns most of it, and it would be best if you and your fella were a good few miles away by the morning. There ain't nothin' I can do or say to stop Bud coming after you.'

'You could keep him locked up.'

'Yes, ma'am, I could, and wind up in the cell myself.

66

I only wear this star because Bud says so.'

'In that case have a dance with me and enjoy your last evening on earth!'

The sheriff didn't know whether to laugh or not, but he did enjoy the dance with Sherin. With Bud out of the way, the atmosphere was lighter, the drink flowed, the dances got increasingly wilder and everyone had a good time. The only group that bothered Trey was the table of three pokes that he'd first noticed when he entered the saloon. He didn't like the way they kept looking at Sherin. Maybe they were filled with admiration at her antics, and although they were repeatedly invited by available ladies not one of them got up to dance.

Long after midnight, the saloon emptied out after a grand night of dancing and drinking. Folk dispersed merrily and noisily to their abodes, while Trey and Sherin walked back to the hotel arm in arm.

'Quite a night,' Trey remarked with understatement.

'The best is yet to come,' Sherin said, squeezing his hand.

'I'm feeling real tired.'

'I know.'

Suddenly, too late, Trey had a horrible feeling that he'd been here before. 'Oh God,' he said. 'Sherin? Not again.'

'Don't be silly, mister, I wouldn't pull that one again.'

But by the time they were in the room and Trey had gallantly settled in the chair, pulling a blanket up to

67

his chin, his eyes started to swim and there was a buzzing noise in his ears, like he'd drunk a bit too much, but he hadn't, he'd been very careful about that. Only he hadn't been careful enough about exactly what he was drinking.

'Sherin, you've done it ag. . .'

She began to look concerned. 'I've done nothing.'

Trey's eyes went all blurry and his head started to swim. Vaguely he saw Sherin slip out of her dress and throw it over a screen, she was wearing something short and black with laces and ribbon and she was walking towards him, frowning, with her arms outstretched.

It was late morning when Trey finally woke. He had no idea where he was. He sat up in bed and looked round the room. It all gradually came back to him, some of it at least. But it puzzled him as to why he was sleeping on the edge of the bed and not plumb in the middle as he usually did. He stroked his chin, it was rough with stubble. Then he recalled he hadn't had a shave for a while. Why not? Sherin. It was her fault, she'd said not to have a shave. She liked the stubble. And where was she now?

Hell, where was she? Where were his dollars?

It all dawned on him much too slow and much too late. Surely she hadn't . . . Maybe she had. He jumped out of bed. The cool air struck his naked body with a shock. He pulled on his longjohns. Sure enough, there was no sign of Sherin. No clothes, no carpet bag, no nothing.

'Damn the woman!' he said out loud. 'What's her game?'

There was a knock on the door. Hopefully it might be coffee and a bite to eat, he was feeling right peckish. He went to the door and opened it a crack to see who was there. The minute he touched the handle the door was thrust back in his face and three men burst into the room all with guns drawn. He recognized the sheriff, Ben and Chad, the latter with a very black eye and mottled cheek.

The sheriff had his gun levelled, but more as a back-up than a real threat. 'Nice try, buster, but you should have left town like I told your ladyfriend.'

Trey wasn't in a position to argue. He put his hands in the air. 'Look, there ain't no need for all this. What's it about? A rough deal in a game of cards?'

'About? About?' Chad said twice, stroking his chin. He lunged at Trey with a sharp upper cut, but Trey was ready for him and blocked the strike. He jabbed at Chad with his right and caught him nicely in the eye. Chad let out a genuine cry of pain.

The sheriff stupidly fired a shot into the ceiling. It brought down large splinters, deafening everyone and showering them in dust and debris. But it did restore order.

'Leave him be, Chad. Listen, mister, we don't want no trouble with you, just put your trousers on and come quietly.'

The scene was almost comical but too serious to be funny. Trey realized he had no option. He dressed hurriedly and was marched down the stairs and out into the street. He was led across to the sheriff's office. Bud was sitting behind the sheriff's desk, a fat cigar in his hand.

'Sad turn of events, mister,' he said, smiling unpleasantly. 'Lock him up, Kyle.'

'On what charge?' Trey demanded.

Bud laughed. 'Cheating at cards.'

Trey was angry. 'This is out of order.'

'Out of your order, maybe. But in mine. Lock him up.'

'You'll regret this,' Trey said over his shoulder, as he was forced at gunpoint into the one and only cell. He had no idea how he could turn the tables, but if he ever did, he swore to make good the threat.

'Kyle,' Bud ordered, 'go back to the hotel and see if you can find the winnings from last night. This tinhorn owes me.'

Trey stood behind the bars, one gripped in each hand and his face pressed close to see what was going on. This was not a happy situation and was beginning to feel horribly familiar. What the hell was Sherin playing at? Was he supposed to wait here until she miraculously turned up and rescued him again? Well, one thing was for certain, unless someone came to his aid, he would be stuck here until they decided he was innocent and let him go.

Unfortunately Bud was not thinking the same way.

Trey was just settling to his reduced circumstances when he heard the sheriff return from the hotel search. He seemed very pleased with himself, sounding like a child waiting for praise from his pa.

70

'We found it, Bud. Right there in the room, guess where.'

'Tell me.'

'Under the mattress, all this paper money.'

Trey saw him throw the bundle on the desk. This was some of his hard-won bounty dollars, which Sherin had stolen from him. Why was she doing this?

Bud got up from the table, he scooped up the notes and walked across to the cell. Trey stepped back, he was taller than Bud but thought it might be dangerous to intimidate this tinpot dictator.

Bud came up to the bars and showed Trey the bundle. The sheriff was standing behind him.

'Do you want to say where you robbed this from. Seems like a lot of dollars for a ridge rider to be playing about with.'

This riled Trey. 'I ain't no ridge rider. If you want to know I'm a bounty hunter and everything I have I own. I'm not a thief.'

'So where d'you get the loot?'

'It's not loot. It's mine.'

'From where?'

Trey was in a spot of difficulty with this question. He was sure it was his, but it might have been from the stagecoach haul that Sherin must have taken. Being a naturally honest man he wanted to say Sherin had given it to him, but this was at odds with what he had just said about owning everything that he had.

'If you want to know the truth, that bundle belongs to the young lady who was with me, the one who lifted your gun.' He enjoyed saying that about the gun

71

because he knew it would remind Bud what a sap he was.

'So it's not yours?'

'No, it isn't.'

Now it was Bud's turn to ponder. He was wondering how much of this haul he could pocket without technically thieving it. He turned to Kyle standing behind him.

'When's the judge due here again?'

'I dunno, he's on circuit somewhere.'

'Reeves Hope,' Trey said helpfully.

'What?'

'He's at Reeves Hope, leastways he was when I last saw him, if you mean Judge Junison.'

Bud was disbelieving. 'You know the judge?'

'In a way. And look if you're thinking of holding me here for trial, I wouldn't bother. It'll end badly for you.'

'For you, don't you mean?'

It wasn't in Trey's nature to keep backing down. He looked Bud in the eye and stared him down until he turned and walked away. 'The judge is a good friend of mine. Don't say I didn't warn you.' It was the first real lie Trey had told.

When he was in the cell at Reeves Hope, Trey had been quite well looked after, though he didn't realize it at the time. Now, given the choice, he would choose to be back at Reeves Hope rather than residing in this pokey little cell with just the thin mattress on the floor and no blanket. There wasn't even a jug of water, and his request for coffee fell on deaf ears. The sheriff was a useless puppet who would do nothing without Bud's permission.

Trey passed a cold and lonely night with only a curse on his lips for comfort. Damn that woman, damn her to hell. He began to think of all the ways he might exact some sort of revenge, but knew in his heart that he would never harm a woman unless in self-defence. As for self-defence, he realized that stupidly he only had himself to blame for his predicament. There was no defence against his carelessness. He never even gave it a thought, he would never have believed that Sherin would do the same thing again and slip some evil concoction into his beer. He wondered what he'd done that night, reflecting on why he found himself on the edge of the bed in the morning, not a stitch to his name again. It was all too bizarre and he didn't want to dwell on it.

The next two days dragged by slowly. He remonstrated with the sheriff, but knew he might as well talk to the wall. Bud didn't show up again in the office. There were no visitors at all, not even people curious to see him, except peering through the window, and when he asked for something to read he was given a pile of dodgers out of the drawer. Now, although that wasn't as good reading matter as the Bible, at least it was something, so he began to study the artists' impressions of the scurvy criminals. Most of them were wanted for bank raids and cattle thieving, a few for murder, and some just described as outlaws with no real category of crime. The drawings varied from believable likenesses to downright fantasy. As he flicked through he stopped on one that looked a bit familiar. There was no name, but those eyes and that big moustache, kind of Mexican but not the eyes, the eyes were too soft. He folded the paper and put it under his belt.

It was almost Biblical that on the afternoon of the third day in his cell, things began to happen. Bud breezed in, with his card-playing friends, a broad smile on his face.

'Hey, mister, you in the cell, good news, the judge is on his way and will be here in a couple days.'

Chad gloated. 'You'd better have a good story ready.'

Trey was not intimidated, he went as close to the bars as he could. 'I warned you. It would be best to let me go quietly. Just let me out, you can keep the money, and I'll be on my way.'

Bud laughed a nasty, guttural, belly laugh. 'Listen, mister, I don't know where you come from, but hereabouts cheating at cards and thieving is a capital offence. . . .'

Trey exploded. 'Don't be ridiculous!'

Bud leant through the bar and jabbed a finger in Trey's chest. 'Listen,' he said again, but Trey was too fast for him. He caught Bud's hand and pulled his arm through, forcing Bud's body up against the bars. Trey swiftly pulled the captured arm down over the cross bar and Bud was pinned tight. With his other hand he reached for Bud's gun-belt and lifted out his pistol. Bud's face was squashed against the cell bars and Trey placed the barrel of the gun fair and square on Bud's temple.

'Now, you listen to me,' Trey began, breathing heavily from the effort of the struggle. 'If I'm being held for a capital crime, it will occur to you that I have nothing to lose by pulling this trigger.' He pulled back the firing pin to make his point. It clicked satisfyingly.

Trey was back in charge of his destiny. 'Sheriff, can I make a suggestion? First, unlock this cell door. Then go and collect all my gear, saddle up my horse, and bring it back here. Make sure the Winchester is in the scabbard. Leave nothing behind, and bring another horse for your friend. Any funny business and Bud's brains will decorate your office wall. Now get a move on. Bud must be hurting in all sorts of places.'

The cell was unlocked, but Trey kept Bud pinned to the bars. The sheriff left, the atmosphere was tense, Chad and Rick could do nothing but watch. Ben managed to slip out of the door.

'Now listen good, Bud,' Trey continued in a menacingly hushed whisper, 'if you so much as try to track me or raise a posse or do any such thing, I will show no leniency and you will end up dead, do you understand? For all your posturing you are no match for a professional, you are nothing more than a jumped up noise, a big pig in a little pen, but it cuts no bacon with me. Give my regards to the judge when you see him, and take my advice, stay in your own slimepit.'

The next moments were quiet and very tense as the four of them waited for the sheriff to return with Trey's mustang. The minutes ticked by particularly slowly marked by the heavy tick-tick of the office clock. At last, the sound of horses and footsteps. The next

75

moment the peace was shattered by a bullet smashing through the office door and thudding into the wall. Chad and Rick ducked for cover, Trey held steady, keeping the gun pressed into Bud's temple.

There was a moment's respite, then the office door inched open.

7

The sheriff came in crouching low. He wasn't holding a weapon and was almost crawling on his hands and knees. He saw Chad and Rick on the floor, then looked towards the cell and saw Trey still holding Bud.

The sheriff was sweating. 'Gee, that's a relief.'

Bud managed to speak, but he almost screamed with fear. 'Kyle, what the hell is going on? You might have got me shot.'

'It was an accident, Bud, I don't know who fired it.'

Trey was calm. 'Well you'd better make sure it doesn't happen again. Get out there and warn them off.'

The sheriff slid back outside. He spoke to the crowd.

'Folks, Bud ain't hurt but if another shot is fired you'll put his life in danger. They're coming out in a minute. Don't do nothin' rash.'

Trey took the opportunity for a dig. 'Hey, Bud, did it occur to you someone might have fired hoping I'd put a bullet through your brain? Now, where is Ben?

I'd watch that one if I was you.'

Bud made no reply.

Trey waved the gun at Chad and Rick. 'You two get outside and keep out of the way.'

Trey untangled Bud from the bars and walked him across to the door. Slowly they went outside onto the boardwalk. It was bright, the sun was still high, flies buzzed round the door. There was quite a good crowd to watch.

Trey pushed Bud down the steps ahead of him and toward the horses. 'Now this is where you have to be very careful. You get on your horse real slow.'

Trey took the reins and looped them over the horn on his own saddle. He kept Bud covered while he climbed up slowly, then swung up onto his own horse, making a show of holding the pistol very steady and aimed at Bud's head. He unlooped the reins and passed them to Bud.

Trey sat upright, proud and every inch the professional. This wasn't the first time he'd extracted his quarry from a difficult situation. Bounty hunters only stay alive as long as their wits let them. Quietly he gave Bud his instructions.

'You ride ahead of me, but only a few paces. The minute there's a gap between your horse and mine, you're dead. Now walk on.'

Mutterings ran through the crowd and they stepped back realizing Trey was not a two-bit greenhorn, but a man who meant business. The two horses moved off slowly and walked down Main Street. Trey never once looked back, someone could have put a bullet in him, if they could shoot well enough, but he figured nobody had the courage and unless they killed him with their first shot, Bud would certainly die. Nevertheless, it was a relief when they reached the end of the street.

'Now you can canter, but remember I'm right behind you.'

Bud put his heels into the horse's flanks and they picked up speed. After ten minutes, Trey moved ahead and brought them to a halt. He had no need to keep threatening with the gun. He came close to Bud's horse.

'I'm going to keep your gun as bounty, a souvenir of Copps Creek. You're free to go now, mister. Remember two things. First, I ain't done nothin' against the law, and second, if I see you again any-where except in Copps Creek, I'll not show any mercy. Now scram.'

Bud said nothing, he turned his horse and left as quickly as he could. A trail of dust showed he didn't stop and he was soon out of sight.

Trey was left sitting on Hoss chewing over the events of the last hour or two. He had no fear of any posse coming after him. He knew they wouldn't dare take him on. He slid down off the mustang and let it munch what grass it could find. He checked his saddle-bags to make sure all his kit was intact. He put on his gun-belt, checked and loaded the Winchester, put Bud's handgun in his saddle-bag, then sat down on a rock and chewed a piece of grass.

It wasn't the last couple of hours that were on his

mind, nor even the last couple of days, languishing in that miserable little cell. His task was to make enquiries about those silver bars, find out about Casey & Co. Was it just a coincidence that the stagecoach taking the bars was robbed just when he caught up with it? There was always somebody who knew about shipments of bullion or cash and such coaches were always a target for bandits. Maybe it had been foolish of the bank to send it without any escort, but an escort would have attracted even more interest. No, the more he thought about it the more puzzling it seemed. Something didn't add up and he couldn't get rid of the suspicion that Sherin knew more than she had said. Why string him along and keep disappearing? It was like a childhood dream of chasing something interesting but waking up before you could catch it.

He wanted some answers. It was time to do some tracking. He needed to find that young woman. He swung up into the saddle, took a long look through his telescope, then set off at an easy trot.

There was a chance Sherin had ridden off in some direction other than Denver, which was still a long way off, perhaps a week's distance or more. Knowing that Trey was going north-west, if she was smart, Sherin would have gone off south, or even back east. There would be no point in looking for a trail in the dirt of the road, he had no idea what her horse's shoes were like or whether there were any distinguishing marks. It's easy enough to pick up the trail of several horses riding together, but to identify one horse on its own is almost impossible.

Lost in thought and looking at the road ahead, Trey's gaze was suddenly arrested by the scuffed up dirt from several horses being ridden close together that had clearly stopped suddenly, stamped about together while the riders were talking, then taken a turning off the beaten track. He pulled up and slid down off his horse. The scuff marks, the broken vegetation, and the freshness of the tracks struck him as strange. There were perhaps three, four or even five riders. This was not a busy road. Copps Creek and Reeves Hope were small settlements on an east-west path but not the main route for the express stages, nor used for much else besides local traffic. So a bunch of riders riding together was noteworthy. But was it worth following up? Sometimes a hunch is all it takes.

'Now then, Hoss, we're going to follow these tracks and see where it takes us.'

The sparky mustang took a sideways look as Trey pulled the left rein. Hoss tossed his head and followed instructions delivered by reins and boot-toes. Trey only ever used his spurs in extreme necessity or when he needed to make a noisy entrance into a saloon.

The trail took them across some very rough country. The semi-desert had given way to more continuous tufts of grass, more dense vegetation with bigger juniper bushes, greasewood and stunted cedars. The ground was still dry but the light turf had been cut by the riders that had recently trampled this track. Following the path, more of an animal track, led him up and down ravines and across a river bed with a springtime flow of deep water. He paused to fill his canteen and let the horse drink, but not too much.

Around midday, came the first real sign of human activity. On a wider patch of ground were the remains of a scuffed out fire. He felt the ground at the darkened centre, it was virtually cold. The ash had been scattered and none of the blackened branches were still warm. He guessed the fire was at least two days old. He poked around and deduced there were four horses tethered separately, each with different distinguishing marks to their shoes. Taking a piece of charcoal from the ground and the old dodger that he had kept, he made a quick sketch of the horseshoes' noteworthy marks. It was a longshot but useful evidence. The way the vegetation was flattened, it was fairly obvious this had been the place for an overnight stop.

A further three hours brought Trey back onto the main track a mile or so from the next settlement. A rough pine board gave it a name: Skerry Halt. It was a loose scattering of timber-framed houses, a main street of no more than a half dozen premises. The scuffed tracks led Trey to the hitching rail outside the one and only saloon. It had a two-storey false front with *Hotel* painted in large letters on a fancy scroll, but when Trey enquired after accommodation he was told there was none.

'But the sign says hotel,' he said to the barkeep.

'Sure does, mister, but I couldn't afford to finish it, that's why I ain't got no stairs and no second floor with the six bedrooms I planned.'

Trey shrugged. 'I guess it's not that busy here. I'll have a whiskey, thanks.'

The barkeep took a bottle off the shelf, pulled out the stopper and poured a drink.

'Did you have a small party of four riders through here just recent?'

The barkeep gave Trey a close look and chewed on his words before letting them out in a cautious kind of way. 'You looking fer someone?'

'Mebbe.'

'Bounty hunter? You look like one.'

'Mebbe.'

'What's your interest?'

'I've been following their trail 'cross rough ground. Seems they were avoiding the main track. Just wondered why.'

The barkeep lightened up. 'Ha! I'll tell you why. I think they caught a bounty, maybe the one you're after. A little Mexican fella. They were having fun.'

'I'm not after any Mexicans. What d'you mean they were having fun?'

'Well, they were drinking a lot, and they kept teasing each other about some sort of reward for the Mexican. They kept making him drink and laughing when he coughed and spluttered. I thought they must be taking him off to jail or something like that. They spent good money drinking spirits and beer. Now if I had folk like that passing through all the time. . . .'

'Do you know where they were headed?'

'No, they didn't say but they kept that poor fella very close, wouldn't let the chap get up and when he wanted to relieve himself one of them went out with him. It was just high spirits, I guess.'

'Was he shackled? Did they use any names?'

The barkeep frowned. 'Names?'

Trey pressed. 'Yes, did they call each other by name?'

'I don't remember.'

Trey was becoming exasperated. 'Do you remember anything else? Was there a woman with them?'

'Woman? No sonny, there weren't no woman, just the four of them.'

Trey knew he was flogging a dead horse and more than likely that party was nothing to do with Sherin at all. Nevertheless, it was a pretty big coincidence that four riders acting strangely had recently passed through.

With no hotel room on offer, Trey decided to make tracks and camp out for the night. Reluctantly, he thanked the barkeep for the drink, despite feeling the fellow had been less than helpful. Just as he pushed through the door the barkeep called out after him.

'They did say something about one of the horses having lost a shoe.'

At last something useful. Trey left the saloon and walked across to the livery. Whatever a small town doesn't have, one place you can be sure of finding is a stable selling feed and blacksmithing services. The sound of hammering meant there was someone at work.

'Howdy,' Trey said to the young man standing by the fire. 'Did you shoe a horse for a group of riders earlier today. Or yesterday maybe?'

'No sir, I did not. I haven't done any shoeing at all.'

'You didn't see four riders then?'

'No sir.'

Another dead end.

The young man took a bar out of the fire and started hammering it. He stopped briefly. 'You could ask my pa. I wasn't here earlier, maybe he knows. He's across in the saloon.'

'Thanks,' Trey said, but underneath he was seething. This was just typical of a small rural community playing their cards close to their chest. He wondered if it was deliberate or if such people really were without much gumption. He walked back into the saloon, trying to contain his frustration.

'Back again?' said the barkeep. 'Another drink?'

Trey wasn't interested in drinking, he was losing his patience and came straight to the point.

'Who's the blacksmith?'

A man sitting just beside the counter turned round. 'You need something?'

'Information. Did you shoe a horse for those four riders.'

The man stared blankly at Trey while pushing his empty glass across the counter. The meaning was obvious, but Trey had had enough of their games, he pulled his gun and fired two shots into the ceiling.

'Did you?' he said loudly when the noise had settled and ears had stopped ringing.

He saw the barkeep stoop behind the bar, the usual movement to pull out a shot-gun that most bar counters had stowed beneath them. Trey levelled his gun at the barkeep.

'Hands flat on the top, mister. Now!'

Trey went up to the blacksmith. 'Well?'

The blacksmith had beads of sweat on his forehead. He raised his hands slightly, submissively, big fat black-smith's hands. 'No need for that. Sure, I shoed a horse, earlier today, belonged to the one called Gonzalez.'

It was the continual identification of one of the men, the hostage maybe, as a Mexican, which made Trey think. He pulled the dodger out of his pocket and unfolded it on the table.

'Is this the Mexican?'

'Maybe.' The blacksmith admitted it was possible. 'And I just remembered something else, they said it was a long ride to Staithes Cross and would I check all the other shoes. They were all right, nothing loose. They paid in coin and rode off.'

Trey holstered his gun. 'Staithes Cross. Well, gen-tleman, I'm sorry that was such hard work squeezing stones for blood. Luckily I didn't have to shed any real red stuff.'

He turned away calmly and went out of the door, mounted up and rode off. The last of the daylight was beginning to weaken. There was just enough light to find the hoof prints from the four riders, especially as one of the prints was quite clearly a well-defined new shoe. It was likely they had ridden hard during the day despite a long stop for a bout of drinking, and had probably turned off into the rough to camp overnight. There'd be little hope of finding them, unless by the slimmest of chances, smoke from a camp-fire could be seen in the night sky. However, there was one thing that Trey thought was in his favour.

Four riders would have little to fear about being ambushed and robbed, nobody would think of taking on four gunmen. So they were unlikely to go very far off the beaten track nor be too careful about hiding their overnight camp. With a bit of luck they would build a good-sized fire to last through the night and with a really good spoonful of luck it might just show up in the dark. Fortified with these thoughts, Trey set off to follow the tracks towards the setting sun. Taking out his telescope, he scanned the horizon. Was that a thin plume of smoke going straight up into the sky? Yes, it was! It certainly was, and about an hour's ride at a rough guess.

'C'mon Hoss, we've got work to do.'

Using the smoke as a marker, Trey was able to keep himself on track until the last of the daylight shrunk away into darkness. However dark the night sky, there is always a thin paler band on the horizon where land and sky join up. The smoke then showed up against that as a dark streak and was easily picked out with the telescope. Distances become less easy to judge at night and his progress was slowed so the mustang could pick his way carefully across the rough ground.

It might have been something more than an hour that it took the nimble horse to cover the distance, but as soon as Trey was within a couple hundred yards of the fire he pulled up, slid down and tethered Hoss. He debated whether to take the Winchester but decided against it, knowing he would need to crawl on his belly to get near enough to the camp. But he did take Bud's six-gun as back-up and secure it under his belt. Twelve bullets would be enough if gunfire broke out. Six was too few.

By now, there was a very visible glow with the occasional sparks rising on the hot air. Trey figured any unexpected noises would be hidden by the cracking of the branches on the fire. But he needn't have worried about that. As he got nearer, the sound of voices singing loudly, accompanied by a reedy mouth organ, would have hidden almost any slithering, scuffing or rustling noises. What he needed was a good vantage point from which to observe the assembled company. Using the cover of the singing, he got as close as he dared without disturbing the horses. They were tethered to low bushes, and there were four of them.

Skirting to the opposite side, away from the horses, Trey found a slightly raised hillock that gave him as good a view as he was going to get. The four figures were well lit by the leaping flames of the fire. More wood was chucked on and the sparks leapt high into the air rising in a swirl of smoke. The singing paused every now and then for the mouth organ to play a short piece and then the next verse hit the night sky. Trey could partially see the faces of three of the figures, although two of them were in profile, and of the fourth person he could only see the back. Perhaps that was the Mexican, because none of the other three looked like the drawing on the dodger. Unless . . . what if? What if there wasn't any Mexican, what if. . . .

He would have to move his position to see the face.

He retreated on his belly and shuffled round the camp until he could creep in closer. His heart missed a beat. Well, well, what d'yer know? This fourth figure was no Mexican, and certainly nothing like the drawing on the dodger, except for the eyes, those soft almond-shaped eyes sparkling in the firelight. Of all the deceitful, dissembling, conniving, underhand . . . his blood began to boil.

8

So, this is what it had come down to. Who were these three men with 'the Mexican', and why was Sherin posing like that? The information from the barkeep at the saloon had suggested the Mexican was under close guard and hadn't been allowed out of the sight of the other men. But, clearly unmasked, Sherin now seemed happy enough to be sitting here by the campfire singing songs with them. Why the disguise when travelling? He'd had his suspicions all along about Sherin being the Mexican. Disguised with that big droopy moustache, she had rescued him at Reeves Hope looking like a Mexican. There'd be some explaining to do when he finally caught her on her own.

But there lay the difficulty, how was he to get her on her own? He sure wasn't going to interrupt this singalong, there was no knowing how that might end. Who were these three men with her? While puzzling that, he suddenly noticed one of them had his arm bandaged up. Was that a massive coincidence or could that be the bandit he had winged in the stagecoach hold-up? Could it? Suppose it was, could these three men and Sherin be bandits? They were certainly all in it together. Sherin, a ridge rider? Well, she seemed to know the area pretty well, those tracks, that hotel, and she had a carefree attitude to money. Could that dodger of the Mexican really be Sherin?

As usual, none of it was making any sense, except that he'd found her again, and this time, whatever the other three men were up to, he wasn't going to let her out of his sight. So what to do now?

The singing stopped. Trey lay perfectly still and scanned the situation. The fire was burning brightly, the aroma of roasting meat was in the air, the horses stirred, and that gave him an idea. He slipped away from the camp and went back to his horse. It was now a waiting game, there was nothing he could do until the camp settled down for the night. He relieved Hoss of the saddle, used it as a pillow for himself and began to doze.

He was woken by the bark of a fox that had unexpectedly stumbled across Trey and Hoss, letting out a yelp of surprise. The darkness was thick, almost impenetrable, and apart from the fox, it was as quiet as the grave. Trey sat up, for a moment unsure of his whereabouts. It was cold, perhaps a little after midnight, and now was the time to act on his plan. Shaking his limbs to get the blood flowing, he took his knife out of his boot and once his eyes had become fully accustomed he moved silently in the direction of the camp.

Taking the greatest care to step slowly and cautiously, to avoid cracking any wood or making any sound at all, he came quietly to the four horses. Someone had stacked the fire before they turned in and it was still heaped with fuel topped with a skimming of tightly packed turf to keep it burning slowly through the night. Fortunately, the moon and stars gave off enough light to see the hobbles on the horses. Very quietly, Trey, making soft snorting noises to keep the horses calm, cut the hobbles on two of the horses. He couldn't guarantee that they would feel inclined to walk off, so he took the mane of one and started to lead it away. It worked, the other free horse followed. He walked them very slowly back to Hoss. He saddled up and with gentle coaxing he attached the two horses to a rope, which he secured to his saddle-horn. Still fearing to make a noise, he stroked Hoss's flanks gently with his heels and they moved off in the opposite direction of the camp.

It wasn't Trey's intention to keep the horses, but on reflection, if the men with Sherin were bandits then it was legitimate bounty. When he decided that enough distance had been put between the camp and himself, he thought a short nap would be in order. He unsaddled, hobbled all three horses, unrolled his soogan and settled to a couple of hours' sleep.

However, the sun was well up when he was eventually woken by the snorting of the horses. It was time for more tracking.

Knowing it was important to locate the camp again, Trey had made careful note of the stars when he came away with the two horses. Before he settled for the sleep he marked the direction with an arrow of dead branches. He was glad he did as the landscape now looked very different in daylight. Fieldcraft is something he'd learnt during the war with skirmishing parties, and since becoming a bounty hunter the skill had become well honed. He'd travelled further away from the camp than he thought and it took him half an hour to come across the remains of the fire. It was still smouldering and they hadn't bothered to kick it out properly. Looking at the ground where the horses had been hobbled he was delighted to see that his plan had worked well. Two horses had left the scene and they were both well laden, it would be easy to follow their deep prints. Not only that, with two riders up, their progress would be slow. Without a doubt they'd make for the next town and hope to acquire two more horses.

Riding to the top of the nearest higher ground, Trey took out his telescope and scanned for the next settlement. It was there, a long way off, a small scattering of buildings. Not a big town, but just what he was hoping to see. Casting his telescope left and right across the intervening space, he spied out the main road. The distance suggested Sherin and her party would hit the town before nightfall, and probably stop there or nearby.

Trey marked out his route with significant clumps of trees, waymarkers on the horizon and the position of the sun. It was roughly a straightforward north-westerly route. There was no hurry. He didn't want to reach the settlement before dark and with a bit of luck, he'd catch up with Sherin at last. Then he looked at the two extra horses. He really didn't need the encumbrance, nor the problem of feed. It would be humane to set them free and let them fend for themselves. Relieved of their saddles and harness, discarded near the remains of the camp fire, the two horses wandered off. Hoss was also glad to be free of them and taking a leisurely walk.

At length the sun went down and day turned to night. Hoss, of course, could see perfectly well, while Trey had to trust his mustang to stick to the path. At length, the outline of the little township, a place called Binney, became visible against the night sky. Trey would like to have ridden up to a saloon, dismounted and got himself a hot meal and a beer, then check in for a room and a bath. None of that was possible. So he made a very quiet entrance to this quiet little place. He steered Hoss round to the back of the hotel, the largest building in the street, two storeys high and a name board on top. He slid down from the saddle and hitched Hoss to a tree sufficiently far away from the building. This was not a social visit. This was work.

Checking his six-gun from force of habit, he slid it back into the holster, adjusted the knife in his boot and removed the Winchester from the scabbard. Although his eyes were nowhere near on a par with Hoss's for night vision, they were at least accustomed now to the dark. There was, in any case, hardly any light on the roadway except the slivers that managed to escape from closed curtains or dusty windows and an occasional dim flurry of yellow as the saloon door was opened and closed. Besides that, and the one feeble light hanging on the hotel porch, the place was in near darkness, exactly as Trey had hoped.

Crossing quickly and quietly to the saloon, he peered through the window only partially blocked by a piece of cloth serving as a make-do curtain. Surprisingly, there were quite a few people and a lot of noise. A couple of card tables were in operation and a game of dice was in progress. With some people standing and others moving about it was too difficult to make out any recognizable faces. He crossed back to the hotel and looked in through the window. There was nobody behind the counter. Gently he turned the door handle and slipped in very quietly. He stepped very carefully on the floorboards hoping to remain silent and peered behind the counter. The register was just there and open. He didn't need to read anything to see that only four names had been entered for this night. He looked at the key board; all the keys were present, which was no help. Carefully he lifted the register onto the counter. Sherin's name was not there, but one of the visitors was named Gonzalez and the number next to that was seven. Things were beginning to make sense in a strange sort of way.

Back outside, Trey wondered what time the saloon would break up and everyone retire for the night. He didn't want to risk looking through the saloon window again, it was important that nobody should see him. There was no point checking the livery for horses, two at least would be stabled there for the night, the two weary horses each having carried two riders into town. Maybe Sherin's friends had managed to acquire two more for their journey on to Staithes Cross, they couldn't go all that way on two horses. A two-bit town like this would certainly not have any decent mounts ready for sale, except out on a ranch. There was nothing to do now except wait several hours for the town to close down for the night. Reconnaissance having been done and feeling hungry, he decided he had enough time to leave the town, light a fire, brew some coffee and eat some of his supplies.

It would have been a lot easier if his eyes worked better in the dark. But since there was no hurry he eventually found enough dry kindling to get a small fire going, and it doesn't take long for a mug of water to boil. Now with some hot coffee and a hunk of cold bacon inside him, he took his ease while thinking out the next stage of his plan. Sherin was in for a surprise, and at last some answers might be forthcoming.

The worst scenario was that she should confess to being a bandit, that she should admit to disguising herself as a Mexican and going by the name of Gonzalez. If that should prove to be the truth of the matter he'd be torn between turning her in and, and, and what . . . what was the alternative? When he caught a ridge rider he always turned them in. Why would this gang be any exception? He didn't owe them anything. Quite the reverse, Sherin had almost got him hanged in Reeves Cross and again in Copps Creek. He dismissed the idea of having any doubts or any crisis of conscience. She didn't mean anything to him. All she'd done was deceive him, trick him and abandon him. She would get what she deserved.

Satisfied with that conclusion, he rolled himself a smoke and sat back to watch the little fire die down. When it had flickered its last flurry it would be time to ride back into Binney and confront the occupant of room seven.

The night temperature was dropping rapidly and Trey lost patience with the last throes of the dying fire. He jumped up and shook himself down to get the blood flowing, then trampled the remains of the little fire, made sure it was fully stamped out, saddled up Hoss and pulled himself up on the saddle-horn. His foot missed the stirrup on the first attempt, causing him to curse. Hoss wasn't impressed either and jigged sideways.

'Whoa, stand still you fool,' he said, more a reflection of his own carelessness than any fault on the part of the mustang.

On the second attempt, he mounted smoothly, of course, but the incident was indicative of his state of mind. He was already concentrating on the effort that would be required to bring him quietly into room seven. Absent-mindedly, he urged Hoss into a steady walk, relying on the animal finding its way back to Binney. Eventually, with the utmost caution he tethered Hoss a little way outside the town limit and off the beaten track. He marked carefully in his mind the exact point on the main road at which to dodge off into the undergrowth and find the mustang. Preparation for a hasty escape was completely normal behaviour for a bounty hunter.

Using the shadows of the buildings as cover, he soon came to the back of the hotel. The weatherboards, painted a dull grey, stood out quite brightly in the moonlight, the windows of the upper floor being black in comparison. It was then that he wished he'd been more thorough with his afternoon's reconnaissance. He should have gone upstairs and made a mental note of the position of room seven so that he could enter by the window if possible. It would have been achievable, by hanging from the ledge that came round from the balcony on the front of the hotel. However, he had no idea which window was in room seven. So access through the hotel was the only route open to him, and that meant wooden stairs and creaking floorboards.

Moving to the front of the hotel and onto the boardwalk, he began to remove his boots, but stopped halfway, reflecting on the difficulty of running without boots as well as the difficulty of drawing his gun while holding footwear. He paused, then put the boot back on. He would just have to tread very lightly.

The glazed hotel door was thankfully not locked. He eased it open and squeezed through the gap. Glancing at the key board, he could see that several keys were missing. It was too dark to read the numbers on the board and as it was well away from the stairs he didn't want to risk footsteps to check the numbers. He proceeded cautiously up the stairs, one step at a time with a pause in between treads. Even at this distance he could hear at least one person snoring very heavily.

By timing his moves with the snores, he was able to gain the top of the stairs in a relatively short time. He was opposite room number five. Which way to room seven, left or right? He turned to the left and was soon luckily outside number seven. Breathing softly, he checked the number on the door and slowly, very, very slowly turned the handle. Once fully turned he gently pushed it.

Now, he realized his oversight. The door was locked of course. Locked and no possibility of access. He stood there looking at the door, thinking. Then he checked the gap at the foot of the door. He remembered once being able to push the key out of the lock so that it fell to the floor and he managed to get hold of it under the gap. That was an epic capture of a wanted criminal. But here, the gap was nowhere near big enough to get his hand underneath. But there was a thin gap.

The gallery round the upper floor had several carpet runners to deaden the sound of people moving about without waking light sleepers. Maybe one of these might just go under the door. He carefully lifted one of these woven carpets and tried to slide it under the door. It went underneath with a little to spare. He positioned it under the lock. Now he had to push the key out of the lock and hope it fell onto the carpet. It was for a job such as this, that he always carried a thin metal rod in a specially sewn pocket on the inside of his leather waistcoat.

The sound of a metal rod poking about inside a lock is not exactly silent. It took him several minutes to free the key and successfully push it out of the lock. The sound of it falling onto the carpet was carefully timed to coincide with the snoring in the adjacent room. Now all he had to do was slowly pull the carpet back under the door. The gap was too thin for the key to come out with the carpet. When he heard the key knock up against the door he used the little metal rod to slide it off the carpet and leave it next to the gap. He withdrew the carpet. Now using the uneven surface of the floorboards he was able to slide the key along to the widest gap and carefully extract the precious item. At last, he had access to room seven.

Slowly and quietly, he regained a standing position. Very carefully he slid the key into the lock and began to turn it very slowly. Using two hands, he was able to control the moment the lock disengaged and release it without it making the usual clonking noise. He turned the handle slowly, slowly. The door opened just a fraction, and immediately Trey knew the snoring was not coming from the next room, it was coming from this very room that he was about to enter. He stopped at once with the door ajar. What the hell?

All his senses suddenly sharpened. He could see the bed to the left of the door, there was someone in it, but the snoring was most definitely coming from behind the door, to the right-hand side of the room. Sweat was beginning to form on his hands, this was an unexpected problem. He should have thought this through more carefully. The barkeep had told him that the Mexican had been kept under close guard in the saloon, and even accompanied to the outhouse.

Yet they had all been singing along together at the camp-fire. Maybe Sherin was not really part of this gang, otherwise why would they keep such a close eye on her, even to the point of guarding her at night?

Now, if it was indeed Sherin in the bed, with one of the men guarding her, a whole new set of problems loomed before him. There was no time to think this through, he had to act on his instinct, and better to act quickly than hesitate. He opened the door wide enough to go in. The curtains were only partially drawn, allowing enough grey moonlight to outline the scene. He closed the door quietly behind him, locked it silently, drew his gun and approached the snoring man, sleeping in a chair.

9

One thing was immediately obvious. The man in the chair with his hand round a six-gun had to be silenced, Trey could not risk him waking and causing a problem. There was only one choice. He approached silently and buffaloed the man. He groaned and slumped forward in the chair, the handgun dropped to the floor waking the sleeping figure.

'What. . . ?'

It immediately registered as a woman's voice. Trey rushed over to the bed and slapped his hand over her mouth. He watched her eyes open wide, dilating all the while with a terrible fear. He tried to calm her.

'Sssh, quiet, stay calm, it's me, Trey. I'm not going to harm you.'

He gently eased his hand to prevent any bruising, but as soon as the gap was big enough . . .

'What are you doing . . .' was as far as she got before the hand pressed down on her mouth, harder than before.

Trey eased the pressure. Sherin uttered a muffled complaint. He held his finger up and waved it at her to hope she might obey the stricture to silence.

'Keep quiet, not so loud! I'm here to rescue you.'

Sherin shook her head violently. Trey eased his grip, but she immediately began a remonstration. 'You can't . . .'

He clamped her. 'I won't tell you again,' Trey whispered. 'Speak quietly or you will wake everyone and they'll be in here before you know it.'

This time, Sherin had got the message. 'You can't rescue me. You mustn't.'

Trey sat back, *mustn't* was not the kind of thanks he was expecting. 'What do you mean, *mustn't*.'

'It's a long story,' she said, beginning to sit up in bed. She pulled the covers up with her. 'I have to stay with them.'

Trey's brow furrowed. 'Why?' he questioned, narrowing his eyes. 'Well, we've got all night, so perhaps you'd better tell me what's going on. Or I'll run you all in and collect the rewards. First I must attend to your friend.'

He walked quietly over to the slumped figure, removed the man's necktie and tied a secure gag to keep him silent. Although he had stopped snoring, nobody had come to see why. Trey proceeded to use whatever he could lay his hands on and secured the man to the chair. The man's own belt, a towel, and a small tablecloth did the trick. He returned to the bed and sat on it.

'I suppose they were afraid you might run away

again in the night. Just like you did to me, twice.'

'That wasn't my choice,' Sherin said, looking deeply into Trey's eyes. 'You must believe that.'

'Must I?' Trey said. 'I don't think so, not until I've heard the whole story. Now start at the beginning and let me hear it.'

Sherin heaved a mighty big sigh and rubbed the sleep from her eyes. 'It's going to sound a bit unbelievable, but you've got to believe it.'

'*I* haven't *got* to do anything, Sherin,' Trey pointed out with emphasis. 'But *you've* got to tell the truth.'

'Are you sure you want to hear it?'

'I'm sure. Get on with it.'

She sighed again. 'It's to do with my husband . . .'

'You're married?'

'Yes and no. We've never had a parson to make it official, but everyone knows I'm his wife. At least he tells everyone I'm his wife, but he doesn't treat me like one. I'm more of a precious possession. He'd like to put me in a glass cabinet with his other ornaments, but at the same time he turns a blind eye to his men making a play for me and taking liberties. I don't understand it and it's hard to live with. So hard that I'd come to realize that unless I changed things it would always be like that. I'm not a possession!'

'Is he a big man, a bully? Older than you by much? A bad lot?'

Sherin looked down and fiddled with the edge of the sheet.

Trey continued. 'You've no need to be protective of him, it doesn't sound like he deserves your loyalty.'

'He doesn't, but it's hard nonetheless.' She put her hand on Trey's for a moment as if she was seeking reassurance. 'I've not told anyone else these things.'

Trey's heart was beating softly, he couldn't help feeling sympathy for this young woman despite the scrapes that she had got him into, including this slightly bizarre night-time episode. 'Go on,' he said.

'He's a big shot in a place called Staithes Cross, owns lots of land, cattle, horses, has majority shares in silver mines, the railroad, anything and everything that makes money. He has lots of men on the ranch to do the work, but he still sends me out to be amongst them knowing that they'll take advantage.'

'In what way?'

'Oh, it's nothing really, they, well, you know, run their hands over me when I pass by, that sort of thing.'

'And he doesn't care?'

'No, I think he actually watches them and gets some kind of weird enjoyment out of it, but I don't like it. They don't treat me with any respect.'

'How did you meet this man?'

Sherin turned her head away, it wasn't a question she wanted to answer. 'That doesn't matter.'

She paused, Trey waited.

'Somehow you were different,' she said looking directly at him. 'I could tell you were different, respectful, even kind. I hadn't met anyone like you before.'

'So you drugged me and did whatever you wanted.'

'No. Well, yes, perhaps I did. I took pity on you dozing in your chair. You looked uncomfortable.'

105

'So you very kindly took my clothes off and dragged me into bed with you.'

'You had some control over your muscles. And I didn't drug you, they did that. Both times. They slipped something in your drink. Of course, you didn't even know who they were. But two of them were always in the saloons when we were. The one you shot in the arm had to stay out of the way in case you got suspicious.'

Trey put a finger on Sherin's lips to stop her. 'I don't want to know about me and all that. Who are these three men you're with?'

'They're my husband's employees. They've come to take me back.'

'Take you back? You ran away?'

'Hey!' Sherin exclaimed. 'I suppose it was you who stole our horses. You thief, that caused us a lot of trouble.'

'Not half as much as you've caused me. Now, go on, you were running away . . .'

'Not really. Look, it's a long story.'

Trey shook his head. 'I know I said we've got all night, but give me the gist of it and keep it short.'

'I want to get out of the so-called marriage, start a new life. I began to look into my husband's affairs and soon realized something was wrong. It was to do with the silver mines. From all three of his mines the silver was sent to Denver for purifying and smelting. The bars were stamped with his name, Kerne Crew & Co; he was proud of his enterprises and always kept a big solid silver bar on the dining table to impress our dinner guests. We had lots of parties, of course. Well, I came across a book of accounts kept in a completely different place, there was no company name and I knew there was something going on because every other account book was headed Kerne Crew & Co. The columns of figures showed the profit margins were huge, even I could see that. The company was making a lot of money. So, I went to Denver to order new dresses and things, he said I could, but I started asking around about smelting company names. Told people I was looking to buy silver. I had to be careful of course wearing a disguise, and every name I heard I made a note of, but I didn't really know what I was looking for. So I watched and waited. I thought if I could catch him out, get him arrested and sent to jail, I'd be free. I didn't dare go to the marshal in Denver, he was one of Kerne's friends, used to come out to the ranch.'

'Did you know the Casey & Co bars were not all silver but had a lead and clay core with a silver coating?'

'No I didn't. So that's what he was up to.'

'That's why the profit was so high. He wasn't selling silver, it was a lead and clay core of the correct weight then a thin silver coating. That's quite an operation, there's a crooked smelter somewhere doing that for him, in business together, and I guess it's nowhere near Denver, probably miles away. Tell me, was everything else going well with his business?'

'Actually, now you've asked me, I think things were getting difficult. Some men were laid off and I did hear that the railway had failed, some other company had bought the land. And one of the mines was slowing down.'

'How long has that crooked silver operation been going?'

'About a year, from the accounts.'

'So far I'm with your explanation of everything, but what were you doing in Reeves Hope?'

'I decided I had to run away. He sent these three men after me and that's where they caught up with me.'

'That doesn't add up. You've just missed out a whole lot of the story.'

'You said to keep it short.'

'But why Reeves Hope?'

'Trey, I'm a lot smarter than I might look.'

'Convince me!'

'The account book gave me a lot of information. It listed shipments and where they'd gone. A bank in Reeves Hope was one of the destinations.'

'But that's miles away from Denver.'

'Exactly. Just like you said about the smelter. All the shipments went to places a very long way from Denver.'

'So you just picked Reeves Hope to try and get some more information?'

'Yes, I guess so, why not?'

Trey shook his head and pursed his lips. 'A curse on chance. You mean we actually met by the purest bit of chance?'

Sherin was quite serious. 'Yes. Call it fate, if you will.'

Trey laughed. 'It all seems so far-fetched that I've got to believe it. And yet . . . this doesn't explain the hold-up. Why did you hold-up that stage with the shipment. It wasn't a coincidence, was it? I know that stage had Casey & Co silver bars, that's why I was after the stage and why I came across the hold-up.'

Sherin's brow furrowed. 'You were after the silver, too?'

'Yes, but . . . skip that for now. Why were you holding up the stage?'

'I wasn't really. It was these three men that are taking me back to Kerne. I had to go along with it.'

'Well, I'm not buying that bit of the story. So, why didn't you let me hang? Why did you come back for me?'

'I thought you didn't want to hear about you.'

'But why?'

Sherin tilted her head, she was playing the feminine card and she knew Trey was susceptible. She smiled slightly so that the corners of her mouth turned up just a little and the whites of her eyes gleamed a touch brighter in the half light.

'Same reason that you're here now.'

There was a gentle knock on the door. They both jumped. Trey got to his feet and whipped out his gun. He crept towards the door.

The voice outside said, 'Irish, are you awake? I can't hear you snoring.'

Trey flashed a look at Sherin and nodded for her to speak to the man outside the door.

She hesitated. Her eyes were wide with fright. She

whispered to Trey. 'What are you going to do?'

'Leave that to me. Speak to him.'

She called out, 'Keep quiet, Irish is asleep, he's fine.'

'I can't hear him snoring. He always snores.'

Trey went back to the bed and whispered in Sherin's ear. 'Tell him you'll let him in when you're decent, so he can see for himself. Go on. Quickly.'

'Wait, Gambini,' she said. 'Let me put something on and you can come in and see him. He's fine, sleeping like a baby.'

Sherin got out of bed, wrapped herself in the bedcover and went to the door. Trey stood to the side.

Gambini was insistent. 'You'd better be telling the truth, I can't hear him.'

Sherin fumbled with the key, moving it noisily in the lock. Trey wondered if she really was nervous or just playing for time.

In the next moment the door was pushed open as Gambini strode into the room, pushing Sherin out of the way and making for the chair where Irish was bound and slumped. He made just two steps in that direction before the pistol butt made a nasty noise on the back of his skull and his legs buckled under him.

Sherin gasped, she closed the door and locked it. 'Now what?'

Trey started to remove the bindings from Irish.

'Why are you doing that?'

'Listen to me,' Trey began, concentrating on the task. 'What's the other man's name, the one I shot in the arm?'

'Indian.'

'I'll catch up with them in due course. Right now I'm going to make this look like a break-in. Give me some jewellery, anything valuable. As soon as I've gone, go and get Indian and tell him you've been robbed. These two will come round eventually. Make them take you back to Staithes Cross as fast as possible, no more robberies or hold-ups or anything. Just get back to your ranch and wait until I come looking for you.'

'You promise?'

Trey stopped what he was doing. He stood up, hesitated, then grabbed Sherin and pulled her into his chest, wrapping his arms round her. She looked up and their lips met in the hot excitement of a proper kiss. It was Trey's answer to her question. He broke off and slapped her across the face, rough handling her arms and throwing her onto the bed.

'Sorry, but I know you would have put up a fight being robbed and you needed some bruises to show for it.'

Before Sherin could say anything, Trey had opened the sash window, fired two deafening shots into the floor, suspended himself from the window ledge and dropped to the ground. Before he ran off he heard Sherin screaming out for Indian. Running from the scene swiftly and silently, he regained his horse, untethered him, mounted up and made good his escape from Binney.

By the time the sun came up he had put a fair few miles between himself and that little settlement. He stopped to make a fire and brew some coffee. Supplies were running low, he'd stock up in the next shebang that he came across. While waiting for the water to boil he took the jewellery out of his pocket, a necklace and ring. He turned them around in his hand. The gold had a rich deep colour and the biggest jewel in the necklace caught the light like a thousand tiny fires edged in a circle of perfect blue stones, the infinite colour of the midday sky. He closed his hand over the two items and the sheriff's impersonal mission to find the origin of the doctored silver bars had now become a very personal matter.

The coffee, the smoke and the last bit of beef jerky was enough to get him going for the day. He saddled up the mustang, promising to see that he got a good bag of oats the next time they stopped for supplies, to which the horse gave a kind of 'I'll believe it when I see it' look, and off they went. As far as Trey was concerned there was nothing now to hold him back from Denver and the search for Kerne Crew's ranch at Staithes Cross, wherever that might be.

'It's a long dreary ride, Hoss, Denver in three or four days, maybe. Depends how fast you go.'

That depends on the oats, Hoss would like to have replied.

10

Snow-covered Pikes Peak, the great pinnacle in the Rocky Mountains, had for several days been Trey's guiding landmark. Now for the first time, he caught sight of the sprawling metropolis, the biggest town he'd ever seen.

Coming into Denver from the south, the whole spread of this huge town lay before his eyes. Everyone knew gold had been discovered along the South Platte river and hordes of prospectors had been drawn in from all over the country. But that bonanza had long since run dry, eventually costing too much labour for too little reward. Then just as the gold ran out, silver was miraculously traced in the spoil heaps from gold mining. Silver mines were sunk everywhere and now the town was flourishing again. If ever Colorado became a state of the union, Denver would surely shout to be the capital.

What was most surprising to Trey was not the sight of so many substantial buildings but the layers of smoke that drifted across the town from the industri-

113

alized western side. Smoke, noise and the smell were
an assault on Trey's senses. Then a plume of more
smoke seemed to be approaching the town from the
east. Taking out his telescope, Trey saw that it was a
train pulling half a dozen carriages, another lucrative
operation sure to bring trade and wealth to the West.
Then he remembered Sherin saying her husband had
lost a lot of money missing out on a railway venture.
Through such enterprises, fortunes were being made
and lost. It was a veritable playground for corrupt busi-
nessmen and swindlers such as Kerne Crew, a class of
criminal who formed a far bigger barrier to the pros-
perity of the nation than any number of ridge riders.
It was apparently called progress.

It was early afternoon when the town first came into
view. The short shadows on the industrial landscape
cast the buildings into sharp relief. As usual the distance still to travel was deceptive and the sun had
dropped behind the mountains before Trey was close
to the town. A short distance away he pulled up,
amazed at the sight. The sky now descending into
darkness, the town mysteriously began to glow. Riding
cautiously through the streets, the glow seemed to get
brighter towards the centre of the town. Then suddenly the mystery was solved. Rows of street lamps, the
like of which Trey had never seen before. It was an
incredible sight. Instead of dark and dangerous alley-
ways, the centre of the town was wonderfully
illuminated. It was unnatural. Trey turned Hoss and
retreated to the darker outskirts, where he found a
small hotel and saloon that met his needs. Hoss was

stabled in the yard with a well-filled nosebag, while Trey ordered a beef and vegetable pie for his meal.

Sitting at a table with a glass of beer and waiting for his food to arrive, Trey cast his eye round the saloon. The local clientele was exclusively male and rather rough. Trey was aware eyes were scanning him and he knew he looked like a bounty hunter. In accordance with town regulations, he wasn't wearing his holster and sidearm, but he couldn't disguise his all-seeing eyes. Players at a game of cards kept looking nervously in his direction. It was a relief when his pie arrived. But his ease was short-lived. One of the locals got up and approached him.

'New in town?'

'Yes,' Trey replied politely, while concentrating on cutting through the golden brown crust and letting a cloud of steam escape. 'Got here today. A long ride.'

'You're making us nervous,' the man blurted out.

'Why's that?'

'Travellers don't stop here often, they get into the big hotels in the centre. Ridge riders and the like hide in the shadows.'

Trey laughed while forking a good hunk of beef into his mouth. 'So, you're on the dodge are you?' he joked.

The man didn't see the humour of the remark. 'Who says?'

Trey saw that his quip had been misunderstood. 'Joshing, bud, just joshing.'

'So what brings you to Denver?'

'Say, bud, you're mighty inquisitive.'

115

The man pulled up a chair and sat at Trey's table.

Trey now gave him a more searching look. His brows were thick and hairy, there was a short scar under his left eye, his stubble was a couple of days old and his hair was unkempt. His waistcoat had greasy stains where his hands had wiped down the front. His body odour cried out for a hot bath. Trey wasn't taking kindly to the liberty of him sitting at his table uninvited.

Trey didn't want to sound aggressive, but his patience was wearing thin. 'Have you got a problem, mister? My pie's getting cold.'

'You look like a bounty hunter.'

At least it was direct. Trey paused, the loaded fork hung mid-air. 'As a matter of fact I'm on my way to Staithes Cross. Perhaps you know it?'

'Yes, I've heard of it.'

'You been there?'

'Used to,' the man said, turning his head and spitting on the floor.

'Then you might know a man called Crew.'

'Know him!' the man almost exploded with anger. 'Sonofabitch.' He held out his hand to Trey. Trey wasn't sure whether to take it. The man continued. 'See, I knew you were the man.'

'What man?'

'Crew should be hung for what he's done.'

'Listen, chum,' Trey said, stabbing more beef. 'Let me finish my pie in peace, then I'll talk to you.'

The man got up and returned to his friends. Trey settled to his pie and beer, then when he'd finished he

116

turned to the man and beckoned him over.

'My name's Trey Cormac, what can you tell me about Mr Crew?'

The man held out his hand again. 'Anthony Dekker, whiskey?'

He sat down.

Trey nodded. 'Thanks.'

The bartender brought over two glasses and a half-full bottle.

'So, Mr Dekker . . .'

'Ant.'

'So, Ant, what's your connection with Mr Crew? Seems a hundred to one shot that in the first saloon I enter in Denver I might find someone who knows my quarry.'

'More like a certainty. There's a lot of people in this town know Mr Crew and his corrupt dealings. He's a great pal of the marshal, the mayor, the town committee, there aren't many folk haven't heard of Mister Crew. He hired me and lots more like me to start work on a railroad. It was going to Salt Lake City. Surveyors mapped out the land while we put up fences, dug the turf, cut the wood. Two months in, next thing, he rides up on a big white stallion and tells us all we're laid off and there's no money to pay us. Sonofabitch. Can you shoot the bastard?'

'I doubt it. I believe he's well guarded.'

'It's true. The marshal's men look after him. Someone'll shoot him one day. Mind, he's got a pretty wife. She's a real looker. Flighty thing, makes out with all the men on the ranch, so I've heard. Don't shoot her!'

That remark about Sherin and all the men on the ranch hurt Trey. What Ant had just told him wasn't quite how Sherin had put it. He set that aside, trying not to dwell on it. A vision of her flashed across his mind, having to slap and bruise her to make good his escape from Binney. He hoped those three men, Irish, Gambini and Indian, hadn't harmed her getting her back to the ranch. He wondered if they were back there already, and how she had been received. Had Crew shown compassion or mistreated her again? Maybe he'd even punished her for running away, and did he know anything about the hold-up at Reeves Hope?

'Ant, did you ever work at Crew's ranch, or go there?'

'Matter of fact, I did. I was there for a week, helping with the beef. That was before the railroad thing.'

'Did you leave the work or what? Why only a week?'

'The foreman didn't much like me, said I was too pushy. . . .'

That was probably true, Trey thought, judging by the approach he'd made to himself in the saloon, just pulling up a chair and sitting down. But this was good news, Trey might get something useful out of this man. 'Could you tell me about the ranch, the buildings and the like?'

'Sure thing, what do you want to know.'

After several smokes and much whiskey Trey had managed to prise enough detail out of Ant to draw a rough layout of the Crew spread on the back of an old dodger. It was a very profitable evening and although

118

neither Ant nor his friends had ever heard of Casey & Co, smelters, or knew anything about doctored silver ingots they had proved themselves to be a veritable gold mine of information.

More than a little pleased with his progress, Trey overlooked the lumpy mattress, the broken window pane and the creaking floorboards in his bedroom. After all, it was perhaps a good place to blend in with the lowlifes of the town and stay out of the marshal's notice. A low profile was essential when his quarry was such a well-known local figure. So, according to Ant, Staithes Cross was no more than ten miles to the south-west of Denver, approaching the foothills of the Rockies. Settling down for the night, fully clothed – this was not the kind of hotel for taking anything off except his boots – Trey decided tomorrow he must take his mustang on a tour to locate the Crew domain. Then he could start to plan his move.

The lumpy mattress was the least of his worries that night. Sometime after midnight, Trey was woken by a crashing noise. There was a grand commotion going on downstairs. A door was smashed open, followed by the heavy sound of running boots. Grabbing his six-gun from the holster in its customary place hanging from the post by his head, Trey leapt out of bed. He took cover near to the window, keeping one eye on the door and the other trying to see how to ease up the casement.

The window was jammed tight, and so was he.

Doors started banging as the hotel bedrooms were

searched. It was only a matter of time before his door would be flung open. He wished he had some idea of what was going on. He didn't have to wait long. Resistance might prove fatal, so he slipped the gun into the belt behind his back just in time. A boot was planted by the door handle and the door roughly forced open. It crashed back against the wall, the jamb splintering as the lock broke away easily. Even in the semi-darkness, Trey could see he was staring down the twin barrels of a shot-gun with a finger perilously close to the triggers. He raised his hands quickly.

'Hold on! Steady there, buddy,' he said with a perfectly unruffled voice, this was no time for weakness. 'I'm unarmed.'

A gruff voice replied. 'Where's Dekker? You hiding him here. Who are you anyway? You the Cormac in the register?'

'Yes, I'm Cormac. I don't know Dekker and he certainly isn't in here.'

While the intruder was considering the assertion, another man came in with a lamp.

'Check him over Barney, he says he's unarmed.'

'Whoa,' Trey said, dropping his hands and sliding one behind his back, closing his fingers round the pistol butt. 'You got some kinda authority?'

The man by the door thumbed his lapel flashing a badge. This seemed very much in line with how Trey might expect the marshal's men to behave, a law unto themselves despite the civilised nature of this growing town.

By this time Barney had approached close enough

for Trey to grab him. He swung him round forcing his arm up his back and turning him into a shield between himself and the shot-gun. He whipped his gun round and pressed the barrel to Barney's temple.

'Say you ease off a bit,' Trey said, still perfectly calm. 'I don't take too kindly to being woken up like that, to having my door pushed in and my life threatened without good reason. So just lower that shot-gun to the floor and put your hands high above your head or your friend's brains will part company with his head. What d'you say?'

The man with the badge hesitated and he licked his lips. He was thinking what to do.

'I'm not feeling too patient,' Trey advised, cocking the gun with a loud click.

The pressure on his temple was clearly agitating his hostage, his voice was urgent.

'For Gawd's sake, Den, what you hesitatin' fer?'

Den bent down and placed the weapon on the floor and raised his hands towards the ceiling. 'Just thinking, Barney, just thinkin'.'

'This ain't no time for thinkin',' Barney continued. 'Dekker ain't here, so let this gentl'man, have his sleep.'

Trey nodded. 'Sounds like a good deal to me.'

'All right,' Barney agreed. 'No hard feelings, Cormac?'

'None. Take your partner and go. The gun'll be downstairs in the morning.'

He kept them covered as they left the room and watched them go down the stairs. 'Good night,' Trey

121

said sarcastically as they disappeared out to the street.

He closed the door as far as it would despite the broken jamb. For good measure he dragged the chest of drawers across the floor and pushed it up against the door to serve as an extra barricade. He dropped into bed and despite the extra adrenaline running round his body he was asleep before he turned over.

In the morning he observed the damage in the saloon. That too had a door in pieces, rather worse than his bedroom door, and the glass was being swept up by the bartender, whom Trey assumed owned the joint.

'A rough night,' Trey said, to make conversation.

'I've seen worse,' was the dour reply.

'Is Dekker in some kinda trouble?'

'You could say.'

Trey pressed. 'What's he done?'

'Talked to you I guess.'

'What? You mean they were after him for talking to me? Impossible!'

'Nothin's impossible where the marshal's men are concerned. They have spies all over the place. Did Ant say anything disparaging about the marshal?'

'Not really.'

The bartender stopped sweeping and leant on his broom handle. 'Let that be a lesson. You're not from these parts, don't mess with the marshal or his men. And I'm afraid you'll have to leave and find another hotel. It don't do for them to know where you are.'

'All right,' Trey agreed, nodding. 'Thanks for the warning. You'll find a shot-gun in the room upstairs, belongs to the marshal's men.'

Trey went out through the back into the yard, saddled up and rode Hoss out into the street. The morning light was casting long shadows across the buildings. He hitched outside a general store and stocked up on essential supplies – coffee, flour, salt, dried meat, bacon, beans, tobacco, rolling papers, matches and a sack of oats for Hoss. He would be spending the next few days staking out Crew's ranch and the mustang would need more than foraged grass to keep him in peak condition.

Before he set out for Staithes Cross, there was one last task. He hadn't yet got any information on the Casey smelting company, and a few questions around the smelting plants in the west of the town might turn up some information. It was worth a try. Or so he hoped.

What he had clearly forgotten is what Sherin had said about what happened to her when she came into Denver and started asking discreet questions. Trey didn't even know what a discreet question looked like. If he wanted to find out about something he just went right on in and asked. After all, most of his questions began with *Have you seen so-and-so? When was he last here?* or sometimes just plain *Where is so-and-so hiding?* Trey was not very discreet about hunting down his targets.

Having already had a run-in with two of the marshal's sidekicks, Den and Barney, Trey should really have thought twice about the wisdom of venturing into sensitive dealings and blurting out unwise

123

questions. But experience is something that comes with age and Trey was only twenty-five. He wasn't a greenhorn, but he wasn't a veteran either. His wits and quick actions had saved him from the rash inexperience of youth, but experience was about to teach him a valuable lesson.

11

The broad streets of Denver were overflowing with buggies, carts, wagons, horses; every kind of conveyance for goods and people. Trey had never seen so many people coming and going, most seeming to know where they were headed, but others just meandering along the shop fronts. Crowds were accumulating near the station, where a train was building a head of steam. The entire place was fascinating but also very confusing to someone like Trey, for whom such hustle and bustle was outside his imagination. There must be plenty of opportunity here for criminal activity and work for bounty hunters like himself. But Trey had no idea about how a metropolis like this dealt with law-breaking with its own council, court system and the whole panoply of law enforcement.

He didn't have to search out the industrial side of the city, anyone with a keen sense of smell could have walked to it blindfolded. The nearer he got to the smelting plants, the greater the volume of noise, dust and smoke. Smelting is thirsty work and there were saloons on the corner of every block. Trey decided to start his questions in the Mountain Dew, a slightly shabby-looking hostelry.

The noise inside was a good deal louder than the noise outside. A quick glance around the clientele told Trey he had come to the right place. Glasses were clinking and the air was thick with cussing. It was a motley sight. Workers from the plant, hopefuls trying to get work, hangers-on hoping for a break, shifty-eyed conmen and dead drunk down-and-outs. Nobody was carrying a sidearm, and that was probably a good thing. At least the weapons prohibition was being observed. Trey ordered a beer at the counter and sat down with it waiting to see what would happen. He didn't have to wait long.

'Howdee, stranger. Passing through?'

His hunch had worked, he thought he would be approached soon enough. 'Eventually,' he replied, dryly, showing no interest.

'Passers by don't usually stop this side of town. Looking for work?'

'No.'

'Well then, looking for some company?'

'No.'

'Hell, you're not very talkative!'

'No.'

The man got up and walked away. He whistled and his place was taken by a young woman who sat down and put her hand on Trey's.

'You look lonely,' she pouted, with a tilt of the head.

'Can I help.'

'Maybe.'

'There's rooms upstairs if you've five dollars to spare.'

Trey raised his eyes at the price, he'd never been asked for that much. He smiled. 'Not that kind of help, miss. I'm looking for information.'

'Bounty hunting?'

'Not exactly. Do you know a man named Kerne Crew?'

The young lady stood up and walked away. Trey watched her go. She stopped to talk to the man who had already tried to engage Trey in conversation. He came back to the table.

'So, a bounty hunter, eh? And playing it kinda cool. What's your business with Mr Crew?'

Trey noted the use of *mister*. 'Just curious. Heard he's some kind of big shot hereabouts. Got a ranch out at Staithes Cross I'm told.'

'Listen, sonny, nobody just asks about Mr Crew without good reason. What's yours?'

Trey had the good sense to guess he was talking to someone who knew a thing or two. He altered his line of questions. 'I'm looking for a couple of men who work his ranch. Indian and Irish. Heard of them?'

'Guess not. Lots of men work for Mr Crew. We smelt his ore in the factory. Couldn't tell you all the names of his men.'

'Ah well, never mind. It was a longshot.'

'Are they in trouble?'

The man had taken the bait, such a question

showed he had some interest in Crew and his ranch, and maybe he did know those two men. Trey had to decide whether to up the ante, or to ease off. He rarely gambled much for money with cards, but he liked playing people, to squeeze them for information, or just for the fun of seeing how far he could push them.

'There was a stage hold-up and robbery, miles away from here, a witness heard those two names and the name of Crew from the town of Denver. At first I thought it meant a robber crew until I started on their trail and got to hear the name of Crew being someone important in this part of Colorado. So here I am.'

The man laughed. 'Ha! And you think you're going to Mr Crew's ranch to arrest those two men?'

That wasn't Trey's plan but he saw some mileage in it. He also noted the man didn't at once deny they could have been involved in a robbery.

'Is there any reason why I shouldn't?'

The man looked him in the eye. 'Depends if you want to live a long life or a short one.'

It was Trey's turn to laugh. 'That's a good question! But look, you work in the smelting business, tell me, have you ever heard of Casey & Co?'

'No.'

The answer was delivered much too sharply and much too quickly. It was obvious the man knew something, but Trey figured he'd pushed as hard as he dared and decided to leave it at that. He drained his glass. Got up and held out his hand.

'Thanks for your help,' he said. It wasn't meant to

sound sarcastic.

Outside in the warm spring air, Trey climbed into the saddle and decided to head south. Once he'd navigated the many streets, he'd head for Staithes Cross to see the lie of the land both physically and metaphorically. Before he left Denver he stopped at a restaurant for a good steak dinner. Then a few miles from the town, he found a quiet spot where he could have a smoke and let Hoss forage for a meal.

Overall he was feeling fairly satisfied with how things had turned out. It still bothered him what he was going to do about Sherin. It didn't much sound like he could just ride into the ranch and whisk her off. And in any case why on earth did he think he wanted to do that? This wasn't about Sherin, it was about Casey & Co and the deputy's job at Corburg. So why go to Staithes Cross? He'd got some sketchy information about Casey & Co in the Mountain Dew saloon. Surely that was worth following up.

The steak and the sunshine overtook him and he dozed off. It was Hoss that woke him with a loud snorting. It was a sound that meant danger. Trey leapt to his feet. Not more than a dozen yards from where he was standing, a rattler was poised and shaking its tail at the mustang. Something had clearly upset the snake, which would usually slither away. This one was too aggressive. Trey commanded Hoss to stay put while urgently, but carefully, he wrapped his fingers round the pistol butt and drew it out of the holster. His arm came up slowly, very slowly while his body position changed very slightly, then suddenly, bang! Just one shot, Hoss reared as the rattler spun into the air like a coil of rope, falling lifeless onto a bush.

'Well done, Hoss!' Trey said, pulling the mustang's ears and slapping its neck. Hoss shook his head, disclaiming any responsibility for the incident. They were soon on their way again.

It's possible that the sound of the gunshot may have drawn a certain amount of attention to Trey and Hoss as they emerged from the scrub to re-join the main highway. A few riders had stopped to see what was going on and at least one had a drawn rifle for protection. Trey raised his hand to the little group.

'Nothing of any concern,' he called out. 'Just an over-eager snake threatening my horse.'

The mildly curious crowd went on their way. Trey turned to the south and rode on.

'Folk are a bit jumpy, it seems,' he said to the mustang.

Before he could say any more, if indeed he intended to, it was his turn to be a bit jumpy. There were a few carts and several riders on the road, but three horsemen arrived suddenly in a cloud of hoofs and dust.

'Hold it, mister bounty hunter!'

Trey was encircled by the riders with pistols drawn and staring eyes that left Trey in no doubt that he was the centre of their attention. He had no option but to pull up.

'Easy there, fellas!' he said raising his right hand in the air while holding the reins in the other. 'What's this all about?'

'You and your mouth.'

'What have I done?'

One of the riders came closer. 'Asking too many questions.'

'Questions? About what,' Trey wondered, but he knew perfectly well what they meant.

'The marshal wants to meet you.'

'I'm honoured.' Trey had half a mind to ask on what authority but the badge was shining too brightly to be missed and he didn't want to be provocative with the odds so heavily stacked against him. 'I'll call in and see him on my way back.'

'Smart, but nuthin' doin'. Turn round and ride in with us or you'll be resisting arrest.'

'Arrest?' Trey exclaimed. 'On what charge? I haven't done anything wrong. There isn't any law against asking questions.'

'That depends on what you're asking.'

At that moment there was a sudden commotion on the road, a mail coach was approaching them at full speed. The rule of the road was clear enough, mail coaches had priority, and in any case it wouldn't be wise to stand in the way of a coach-and-four at full tilt. It was the smallest window of opportunity, but Trey wasn't going to let it pass. He swung his horse round to the side of the road, whipped his pistol out and shot one of his inquisitors. The man fell from his horse into the road. The mail coach driver tried to pull up, but it was too short a distance and the coach swerved, causing a massive cloud of dust and ran over the fallen rider.

Trey wasted no time in looking on. He spurred Hoss into the scrub, taking full advantage of the swirling dust. A bullet zinged into a tree close by, Hoss gathered speed, there was no way he wanted to be shot in the rump. As soon as he felt himself to be reasonably clear of the scene, Trey pulled up violently, grabbed the Winchester out of the scabbard and dropped to the ground. If anyone was following he was ready to drill them. The mustang, now without its rider, carried on a distance while Trey settled himself into a prone position with the gun trained on the path through the scrub. The undergrowth gave him just enough cover to wait for the inevitable riders who were surely on his trail.

Soon enough, he heard the hoofs, not galloping but hurrying in his direction. His one lucky break was that his two inquisitors had pulled off the other side of the road as the coach ran over their buddy. This had given Trey the vital seconds to get clear. It would appear they hadn't hung around to attend to the rider he had shot, no doubt finished off by the mail coach if not by Trey's bullet.

The time to aim and shoot was counted in seconds, but as the two riders came into view Try fired three shots in quick succession at the first rider. The man was thrown back in the saddle and dropped to the side, one foot caught in the stirrup. Badly impeded, the horse quickly pulled up. The second rider turned and fled. Trey fired again but with no success and the man rode off. He walked across to the stationary horse and looked at the man dangling from the stirrup. It wasn't a pretty sight. Two of the bullets had found their mark and

opened a bloody hole in his chest. His face and cloth-
ing were scratched and torn from the short distance of
dragging. Trey pulled the foot out of the stirrup, the
body fell to the ground and the horse ran off.

Looking down, Trey knew he was in a whole pile of
trouble. This was a very bad turn of events. Briefly, he
reflected on the stupidity of asking all his questions
without some circumspection. He didn't dwell on his
rash stupidity, but he did learn the lesson. He bent
down next to the body and looked at the badge. He
unpinned it from the man's lapel. Now, in his short
life he had nevertheless seen lots of badges when col-
lecting bounties or asking sheriff's for any new
dodgers. He turned this one over in his hand and
looked at it closely. A badly cast fake. There was no
doubt whatsoever that this wasn't anything to do with
the marshal in Denver, at least not up front. It looked
good from a distance, enough to fool a law-abiding
citizen, and it had nearly fooled him. Thank goodness
for his instinct and the lucky mail coach.

It was also a relief to know that he hadn't killed a
lawman, probably just two hoodlums, or maybe men
in the employ of Crew and his shady operation. Either
way, it was a lucky escape and a good lesson learnt.
Now to find Hoss. He whistled and whistled again.
Before too long Hoss appeared with a disdainful look
on his face.

'That was a close-run thing,' he admitted to the
horse. Hoss would just have indulgently raised his eyebrows if he knew how. 'From here on we keep off the
main road.'

Trey pressed his heels into the mustang's flanks. 'Get on, we've still got a way to go.'

The ten miles to Staithes Cross had become fifteen by a circuitous route away from the road, and what with the rush of adrenaline still dissipating in Trey's veins he was glad to see wisps of smoke announcing his approach to the settlement. It had been a relatively short but strenuous ride. Gaining the crest of a small outcrop, Trey took the telescope to his eye and swept across the view. The town was not large, not much more than the little settlement of Copps Creek and all around were verdant pastures, stands of cottonwood, clumps of pines, a gleaming river and a vista away to the foothills of the Rockies. Pike's Peak still stood out in the distance like a sharp pinnacle jutting into the sky. It never seemed to be closer nor further away.

So, this was Crew's land. By all accounts, most of what Trey could see probably belonged to that man. Somewhere down there was a ranch house, and somewhere in it was Sherin Crew. Try as he might he couldn't separate the thought of her from the thought of her husband. One was his quarry, or an adversary at least, and the other . . . the other, what did she mean to Trey? Anything? She was Crew's wife, in all ways but legally, and she made free with his men according to what he'd heard. Not from her of course, she'd put it very differently.

It was an unfamiliar situation. Trey concertinaed the telescope and stroked his chin. There were three things he had to do. Find a place to make a secure camp, find and stake out Crew's ranch house, and talk to Sherin. He bit his lip. Why that last one? Why did he need to talk to Sherin? He was here to find out about Casey & Co, get information on the bum silver ingots, get that deputy's job in Corburg. That's why he was here. Sherin was just a distraction. But however hard he tried, he knew he wouldn't finish this job without wanting to speak to her again.

First things first. A camp before nightfall. This job was going to last a few days and he needed somewhere safe to hang out. When scanning the land with his telescope he thought he'd seen a good stretch of rough forest away to the west, far enough from the settlement and close enough to be in touch.

It was an hour's ride that brought him to the woods and another quarter to find a good spot near running water and plenty of cover from young willows and aspens from where he could see without being seen. It was tucked away behind a screen of pines that would hide smoke from a fire. It was already getting dark and by the time he'd gathered enough wood the sun had sunk behind the mountains to the west and the stars were beginning to appear.

Bacon and beans eaten, coffee drunk, tobacco smoked and the night sky now black, it was time for Trey to drop out of the woods and onto Crew's land for his first reconnaissance trip under the pale light of a great silvery moon. The ranch house was his first target, he had to know where that was located.

Riding around a town at night immediately arouses the suspicions of law-abiding citizens. Trey couldn't risk being stopped and eyeballed, much less being seen asking questions. His lesson on that score had been learnt the hard way. No questions to be asked! From his initial scan of the area he had alighted upon a significant group of buildings to the south of the town and he now headed in that direction. As much as possible, he kept off the main track and made slower but secret progress towards the ranch. It was a lucky hunch.

The gateway that he came across was huge and ornate, but more importantly was carved with the name Crew and underneath *The Bar KC*. This is exactly what Trey hoped to find, this was Crew's place and his cattle were marked with a bar and KC brand. KC? Casey! So that was it! The secret account book Sherin had found was for Casey & Co and that was definitely her husband's swindle. He should have made that connection sooner, at least he'd made it now. He could see the deputy's star on his chest already, Corburg's newest lawman! Things were looking good. Now he knew he needed that account book and then he could prove the connection. It would be far too risky to attempt some kind of robbery, even if he knew where the book could be found. No, he would have to see Sherin and get her to steal it for him. Sherin, so finally she did have a part to play and he would have to see her again. But how? Tonight's mission was accomplished and a plan was beginning to form in his mind.

12

It being close to dawn by the time Trey got back to his camp, he slept well beyond sun up and although he woke from time to time, it was nearly midday before he finally crawled out of his soogan. Hoss had already foraged as much grass as he could within the length of his tether and was waiting patiently for something to happen. It was not a day for happenings, it was a day for watch and wait.

From a vantage point amongst the trees, now that he knew exactly where the ranch house was located, Trey could focus his telescope on the main buildings. At some point in the day, Sherin would surely come out, maybe for a ride or to take a buggy into Denver. Trey had forgotten that half the day had already passed him by and more than likely Sherin had taken an early morning ride some hours ago. But there was still the matter of ranch hands and other comings and goings to watch.

Patience was not one of Trey's virtues but he managed to maintain a vigil through the afternoon and learnt a lot about the number of men around the ranch, or working in the yard. He got a good fix on the buildings. While he was watching there were two deliveries in medium-sized carts but that was all. Nothing that looked important or noteworthy, at least not until late in the afternoon when a rider came out galloping across the fields more or less in his direction. It was Sherin. He was sure it was her.

Suddenly woken out of the monotony of constant observation, Trey grabbed his telescope, taking several minutes to locate the horse and rider as it crossed fields and fences, leaping over gates and ditches making for the open country leading to the forest where Trey was encamped. When he finally got the rider in his glass there was no doubt to whom that flowing mass of copper hair belonged. It streamed out like the horse's tail, although the palomino's tail was a different colour, and it was clear both horse and rider were enjoying the thrill of speed and danger.

Long before they came anywhere near Trey, the pair veered off to the south and were soon lost in the margins of the trees. But it gave Trey hope. If this was Sherin's evening riding route he'd be able to catch up with her tomorrow or the day after and get that account book with the evidence that would bring Kerne Crew to justice and end his crooked operation. More importantly, it might just secure that deputy's job in Corburg and that was what he wanted more than anything else.

The next part of his plan now being envisaged, Trey broke off the observation for the day, made up his fire, and relaxed with a cup of coffee while the beans cooked through and the bacon sizzled over the flames. Despite not having got up until midday, a strange lethargy overcame him after he'd supped and smoked. He put it down to the exertion of the last few weeks, the narrow escapes, the lucky turns and the over-production of adrenaline. All those things had left him a little bit drained, and sleep was by far the best restorative.

He slid himself into the soogan well before the moon was anywhere near halfway in its transit and, deaf to the calls of the owls, foxes and everything else, he drifted off into another world where Sherin was riding the biggest horse he had ever seen. Try as he might, he never quite caught up with it. Suddenly it stopped while he was pursuing it and a flurry of pages full of columns and stuffed with figures came fluttering through the air. Sherin and her gigantic horse disappeared in a cloud of smoke. He woke in a sweat.

First light was just spreading its fingers through the valley, birds were singing, and aspen leaves were rustling in the morning breeze. He pulled the soogan up to his chin, rolled over and went back to sleep.

At last, much revitalised from so much rest, Trey felt himself again on top of the world and in peak condition. So much so that when he finally got himself up and fully dressed he used a low tree branch to flex his muscles, pulling himself up to the count of forty and feeling all the better for it.

There wasn't much to do for the day, he was waiting until Sherin's afternoon ride when he would try and catch her. So in the meantime he decided to give Hoss some exercise by riding out west through the forest and into the open land, to explore the wide expanse of the foothills to the Rockies. Maybe he could shoot a rabbit for dinner. There was something very satisfying in just riding through open country without much of a care in the world. His current mission was very clear and almost sewn up. He had no intention of taking on the Crew operation by himself, but with the evidence of the account book and the fake silver ingots a federal marshal would take on the case, although not the one in Denver.

Then what of Sherin? What did he feel for her? Anything? Nothing really, well nothing substantial. Her life here in Staithes Cross was one he didn't want to get involved in. There was no place for him in her life, nor for her in his. Certainly he wanted to ask some more questions. What about that Mexican dodger and her disguise, what was that all about? Her story about the hold-up near Reeves Hope still didn't add up. But, on the other hand, was she really in any danger, did Crew actually abuse her, was she really forced to go with ranch hands? It was all too complicated. Yet, he couldn't forget she had ridden back to save him from the judge and jury, saying she felt something for him. No, she wasn't really serious, but he'd promised to meet up with her in Staithes Cross, so here he was. Now he felt very near to accomplishing everything.

Meandering along, deep in thought, he'd arrived at a rushing stream and allowed Hoss to drop his head and drink.

'Stop right there, and raise your hands!'

It brought Trey back with a crash into reality. He put his hands in the air without looking behind. Any other movement might be fatal.

'Who are you, stranger? You're trespassing. This is Crew land, you shouldn't be here, can't you read?'

'Sorry, mister, I didn't see any signs,' Trey said. 'There wasn't any fence.'

'Don't mean it ain't private land, just cos there ain't no fence. Turn round and let me see your face.'

Trey was thinking fast. He didn't want to appear like a trespasser. He didn't want to be shot in the back, nor in the front. Was this a way to get to meet Mr Crew or was that a risk too far? What should he do?

'What's your business out here?' the man asked waving his gun menacingly. 'Poking around on private land.'

'I've already said I didn't know it was private land.' It was time to gamble. 'But as it happens I was hoping to meet Mr Crew, and if you say this is his land then I must be in the right place.'

This temporarily threw the other man, he hesitated. 'So what's your business?'

'I'm a prospector,' Trey said on the spur of the moment. He was gambling on the man being just a ranch hand of no great significance, a boundary rider nothing more. 'I've heard there's plenty of silver in these hills and I'm looking to do a deal.'

The man laughed. 'Mister Crew has all the silver he needs. He doesn't do deals with down-and-out prospectors. Where's your equipment anyway?'

141

'In Denver, with my team. Look, do I get to meet Mr Crew?'

'Why didn't you ride into the ranch off the road like anyone else, before poking around out here?'

'Like I said, buddy, I didn't know this was private land.'

It sounded convincing. It looked like Trey had won the argument for the moment.

The man rode forward. 'Hand gun, butt first, then the rifle and keep your hand away from the trigger.'

Trey handed over the guns. All that remained was the knife concealed in his boot. He was made to ride beside the other man, who kept his pistol in his hand all the time. Trey's imagination was working as fast as it could. What should he do? Did he really want to meet Kerne Crew like this? He'd be found out very quickly, he knew nothing about prospecting except that you needed a shovel and you should be carrying rock samples for assay. What on earth was he going to say to Kerne Crew that would make any sense about being found trespassing on his land, even by mistake? He could think of nothing, so continued beside the boundary rider hoping some inspiration would arrive before they reached the ranch. He toyed with the idea of mentioning that he knew Sherin, but on balance decided against it. It might be a card he would have to play later. An idea was beginning to take shape.

Although Trey's ride into the foothills had taken him some distance away from his camp above the Crew ranch, the boundary rider took him back down a very different track that brought them out onto the pasture land much more quickly. It seemed all too soon that they were in the yard and dismounting.

Just as he slid down off Hoss, still covered by the rider's pistol, though no longer pointing directly at him, he noticed the palomino being held in the yard, saddled up and ready for its rider. It must be near the time for Sherin's afternoon ride. Trey hoped he wouldn't see her. What if she came out and said hello, or in some way acknowledged him? It would raise all sorts of questions.

Sure enough the door opened and out she came, looking stunningly beautiful in her riding gear, her hair tied into a ponytail and her riding britches tight on her legs. Trey's heart skipped a beat and his eyes widened. How such a moment devastated all the good intentions and clever plans that had been formulating in the last hour. All shot to pieces in one moment; the moment that Sherin looked him right in the eye and he knew she meant more to him than he dared acknowledge.

Thankfully she said not one word nor gave any sign of recognition to anyone nearby. But that look drilled deep into his heart, and there was nothing he could do to stop it. He looked away quickly.

'In,' was the only word the boundary rider spoke, accompanied by a prod in the ribs with the pistol barrel.

Trey went up the steps and stopped in front of the huge double doors crafted out of solid oak and studded with big black bolts. The wrought-iron hinges reached more than halfway across the doors. One was opened for him and Trey was pushed forward. Inside the door was another man, Crew was well guarded, it seemed. Trey was taken through a succession of rooms until they came to a closed door. His escort guard knocked.

'Come.'

The escort opened the door.

The boundary rider spoke up. 'A trespassing prospector, Mr Crew. Found him riding the foothills. Says he wants to meet you.'

Kerne Crew looked up from the desk. He had a shifty face, eyes a bit too close, mouth a bit too mean. His shoulders were broad and he was well muscled under his shirt. There was a lot of grey in his beard and the furrows on his brow made him look much too old for Sherin. Perhaps there was truth in what she had said about him abusing her. He certainly looked mean enough.

'Leave him here. Get out, both of you.' It was a good indication of how he treated his employees. Maybe he treated his wife the same way.

Crew ran his eyes briefly over Trey. 'You're no prospector. What the hell were you doing on my land?'

Trey put his hand up to acknowledge the question. He knew that the only way to deal with overbearing bullies is to respond in kind.

'That's right, I'm no prospector, I'm a bounty hunter.'

'Bounty hunter! You're in the wrong place. Nobody here is on a dodge. Get back to where you came from.

144

They'll give you your guns on the way out.'

Trey sat down in a chair facing the desk. 'What about Irish and Indian or Gambini?'

'Get out!' Crew shouted.

Trey sat perfectly still. His heart was thumping, but he knew his defiance would be foreign to Crew, who was more than likely always obeyed without question by a fearful workforce. Resistance to his orders was something new.

'Get out now!'

Trey smiled. 'I don't think so. Not unless you want a lot of trouble to come your way.'

'Listen, sonny. Nobody threatens me like that. A snap of my fingers and your hide will be hung out to dry before you can stand up.'

'That won't avert what's coming to you.'

'What d'yer mean, sonny? You got some information for me?'

Trey was thinking rapidly. What card should he play first. Link Sherin to the Mexican on the dodger, claim an arrest on Irish, Indian and Gambini for the stage robbery, or strike at Crew's jugular with mention of doctored silver ingots?

'No information *for* you, but *on* you. In fact, too much to let it pass. But I'll do a trade with you, if you like. I'll drop my investigation into Casey & Co in exchange for your wife.'

Trey's heart missed more than one beat. He had never intended to say any such thing and had no idea why he had blurted out such a ridiculous deal.

Crew was visibly shocked. Then he laughed out

loud, a long belly laugh. 'What?'

Having started, Trey was not going to be intimidated by this man. 'I know all there is to know about your operation, Mr Crew, and I have a federal warrant to bring you in. But I'll give it to you to tear up in exchange for your wife. She's not really your wife, is she, never was a proper ceremony was there? You know she wants to leave you. She'd already run away, didn't she? To Corburg. She was part of the robbery with those three men I mentioned, something to do with your doctored silver ingots.'

'Stop! You're making a big mistake. I don't know anything about Casey & Co, never heard of them. Yes, my wife, Sherin, did go off a while ago, something to do with a bank in Corburg, but I don't know what it was about, she didn't tell me the detail. And as for those three men you mentioned, I've never heard of them. I'm a very busy man, I haven't got time to ask everyone about everything they're doing.'

'Not even your wife?'

'What's your name, sonny?'

'Cormac. Trey Cormac.'

'And you're a federal marshal?'

'No, I didn't say that. I'm a bounty hunter with a federal warrant for your arrest.'

'And just how do you propose to execute that?'

'If, as you claim, you've nothing to hide, you'll ride into Denver with me tomorrow and give yourself up to the marshal.'

Crew laughed. 'I'll go one better than that. Meet me here tomorrow at noon. The marshal will be happy to see you!'

This had gone too far. Trey's bluff was going to turn a small prevaricating advantage into a massive defeat. His entire scheme had gone up in smoke because of some rash, stupid deal about trading Sherin. He'd unwittingly played all his cards without winning the pot. How could he get out of this? At least it sounded as if Crew was going to let him walk right on out, get his weapons and leave the ranch peacefully. Really? After everything he'd said and all the information he'd given, without the slightest bit of a bargain in return. Crew was just going to let him walk out and come back tomorrow to face the marshal? This was unreal. And what on earth had made him suggest a trade between a non-existent warrant and Crew's wife. Had he really lost his head? Or just his heart?

Crew waved his hand at him and looked down at his paperwork. 'Go on, get out!'

Trey didn't need to be told twice. He turned and went to the door, opened it and left the room. He retraced his steps towards the entrance hall to collect his guns. The boundary rider was sitting on a chair waiting for him. He got up as Trey approached and held out his guns for him. Trey was about to take them when he felt a sudden blow to the back of his head, his legs gave way, his eyes closed, his ears throbbed with a buzzing noise. The floor rushed up and hit him in the face and the world went as black as night.

13

It was night time. Trey could see the stars in the sky but he wasn't by his camp-fire, he was looking through a window. Was he in a hotel? Back in the shabby hotel in Denver? Where was he? He tried to move, he wanted to get out of bed, but he couldn't, his hands were tied behind his back and his legs were strapped together. Gradually things came back to him, then there was an alarming flurry of thoughts. He wasn't in a hotel, nor his own soogan, he was at Crew's ranch. The sonofabitch had never intended to let him go. Now he rued his strategy, all the bluffing and bravado. He realized he had indeed played all his cards and stupidly allowed himself to be fooled into a false sense of security. And paid the price, so now what?

Trussed up like a thanksgiving turkey, there was nothing he could do. His eyes slowly accustomed to the dark. The starlight through the window allowed him to see that the room was very small. More importantly there was no guard sitting in with him. Most likely there was one outside the door. He looked up at

148

the window, it was probably just big enough for him to get through, but he couldn't see any catch to open it. Maybe it was just a pane of glass that let in light without opening. He guessed then that this room was high up from the ground, so even if it opened it would be a hell of a drop. Things looked very bleak indeed and his head was throbbing horribly. He would just have to wait and see.

Dozing fitfully, he slipped in and out of consciousness, unsure whether he was awake or asleep. The sound of a door being opened filtered into his semiconscious state, he was dreaming of Sherin. Someone was whispering. *Trey, Trey, wake up!* but he couldn't pull himself out of the depths.

Then suddenly a hand was on his face, this was real enough, he woke with a start.

'What . . . !'

'Sssh. Keep quiet.'

The hand was soft and warm and his cheek was being stroked. Was he dead? Had he died and gone to heaven, is this what it was like? All that nonsense about angels.

'Trey, it's me, Sherin. How are you feeling?'

Now it was real enough. He wasn't dead, but very much alive. He tried to sit up, but the binding held him fast. His muscles ached unbearably, his whole body was stiff. Circulation had been slowed by the awkwardness of lying bound up with his arms behind his back.

Sherin pulled the flimsy blanket off the bed and began cutting the cords. Trey was now fully awake. As soon as he was released he rubbed his arms and legs and the blood began to ease the pain. At the same time his head was full of questions. But he didn't get a chance to speak. It wasn't that long ago that it had been his hand and Sherin's mouth, how life is full of strange twists and turns.

'Listen,' Sherin began, 'you have to get away or Kerne will see you hang in Denver. He told me all about the meeting and said he's going to lay charges against you. The marshal will be here in the morning to arrest you, and that'll be the end of you. Look, I've got your six-gun here. You might need it.'

He took the gun and slipped it into the back of his belt. His brain was working as fast as it could. 'Did he say anything about Casey & Co?'

'No, why do you ask?'

'When I challenged him, he denied all knowledge of it and it made me wonder whether he was bluffing or telling the truth.'

'What do you mean?'

Trey continued with his doubts. 'He also denied any knowledge of those three men who were with you, Irish, Indian and Gambini. They don't work here apparently. Were you lying, Sherin?

'Of course they work here,' Sherin said crossly. Then changing the subject, she said, 'But Kerne told me something interesting. He said you offered a deal, something about me and a warrant.'

Trey stayed silent, massaging his muscles.

She pressed him. 'Did you?'

Trey was embarrassed by the directness of the question. Up to now there had been a sort of understanding

150

or misunderstanding between himself and Sherin. At one time he thought she was a better prize to win than getting information about the silver ingots and winning a deputy's star. She had said she wanted to be rid of Kerne and hinted that she wanted to be with Trey, or maybe he had misread all that. His experience of women did not yet extend to the hints, prevarications, intricacies and obfuscations of their intimate conversation. In the back of his mind the deputy's job was much more important to him.

The offer to exchange the non-existent warrant for Sherin had just come out as much of a surprise to himself as to Kerne. Had his heart overruled his head? And now, his head was in such a spin he didn't know what to say. Luckily, in one way, but not in another he didn't have to decide.

The door burst open and lamplight flooded the little room, two men came in with the light, guns drawn and behind them the burly figure of Kerne Crew holding the lamp aloft. It was Crew who spoke.

'So. Caught red handed. It was true what he said. Sherin, you little doxy! You thought to run away with this bit of trash, did you? I didn't believe it, but I knew if it was true you'd try and save him.'

'No, Kerne, it's not like that . . .'

'Lying bitch. Take them both.'

One of the men grabbed Sherin and held her fast, the other lunged towards Trey. Instinct kicked in and before the man could grab his arms Trey pulled his gun from behind his back and slammed it into the man's face. He crumpled to the ground with a scream

151

of agony, the metal had cut flesh and broken bone. Fast as lightning, Trey put his boot on the man's neck and held his gun rock steady aimed at Kerne Crew's head.

'Don't move one single muscle, Crew, I won't hesitate. Tell your man to let Sherin go.'

There was a long, tense pause.

Crew sighed. 'Do as he says, Irish.'

'Ah!' Trey exclaimed. 'So here's someone who doesn't work here! Hello again Irish, the last time we met was in a hotel, but you probably don't remember that, you were asleep at the time!'

Irish let go of Sherin and raised his hands. It was a tight space in the room and Trey was taking no chances.

'Sherin, tie Irish's hands with the cord. Now use the other piece to tie this one.'

The man under his boot had passed out and as Sherin bent down to tie the hands, Crew took the opportunity to make a move. He threw the lamp into the room and, turning, quickly made off down the narrow stairs. The lamp smashed against the wall, the kerosene spilled and the vapour ignited in a blast. Trey fired one shot after Crew, pushed Irish aside and headed for the stairs. Irish recovered balance and awkwardly with his hands tied, ran for the stairs.

Sherin stopped to pull the other man to safety out of the room then grabbed the blanket and started beating out the fire. She was too occupied with the task to notice another three gunshots. When she had smothered the fire, she almost tumbled down the

152

stairs and was greeted by a sorry sight at the foot of the second flight. Kerne was lying slumped against the railings and Irish was hunched on the floor, a large bloody patch on his leg.

Trey looked up as Sherin arrived. 'The fool pulled a gun on me. He missed and hit Irish in the leg. I fired twice and I'm afraid he's dead.'

'Kerne's dead?'

'Yes. I had no choice.'

'Good riddance,' Sherin said. 'He won't be missed. You'd better go and get the other man upstairs, it's Indian and he's going to need the doc.' She looked at Irish, his bound hands clamped to the wound. 'I guess you do too, Irish.'

Irish was wincing with the pain and gasping. 'Yes miss, your husband never was a good shot.'

'Don't call him that, he was never a husband to me.'

It was late morning before the doctor arrived in a buggy, having been collected from Denver. He signed the death certificate for Kerne Crew and patched up the other two employees.

'What will you do now, Sherin?' the doc asked. 'It'll be strange not having Kerne to run the place, can you do it yourself? We'll miss him on the town council. He was a good man.'

Sherin shrugged. 'Not such a good man as you think, Doc. Now he's gone you should know he was one of the biggest crooks in these parts and a down-right bad man through and through.'

'You shouldn't speak ill of the dead.'

'Listen, Doc. You don't know the half of it. A person has many sides and until you know them all you should hold your tongue. Kerne Crew was a sono-fabitch, he was a mean-minded bully and that's the truth.'

The doc decided not to probe further into the char-acter of the man who was lying under the sheet. 'So what will you do now? Sell up?'

'I don't know, Doc, I need time to think.'

The doc turned to Trey. ''And who are you, sonny? I haven't seen you here before.'

'It's a long story, and you don't need to hear it,' Trey said simply and left it at that.

Later, after the doc had left and things had calmed down, Sherin called all the hands into the ranch for a meeting. She told them straight exactly what had hap-pened and why Trey was standing next to her. She told them about the doctored silver ingots and was glad to discover that none of the employees on the ranch knew anything about it. Trey noticed nobody spoke up for Kerne Crew nor said anything good about him. There was a visible air of relief and when Sherin asked them if they wanted to stay on or leave, only a couple said they wanted to go. The others clearly felt a loyalty to Sherin.

That night, the evening meal was a subdued but not sombre affair. There were some dozen or more hands that sat down with Sherin and Trey to a good spread that cook had prepared. They had just finished eating the fruit when Irish was urged to speak up. He stood up, looking a bit uncomfortable, then banged his fist

154

on the table.

'I gotta speak,' he began, in a loud voice. 'I ain't going to sing no praises for Mr Crew, he was a tough sonofabitch. Personally I'm glad he's gone, I guess we all are, even Sherin. I'm glad she's decided to keep the place running, 'cos, with old sourface out of the way, this ain't a bad place to be and I like working with the beeves. Easier than people! As for you Cormac, you gave me a beating, but I don't bear no grudges. You're a decent man after all and me, Indian and Gambini were only acting under orders.'

He paused for a moment, then got a bit more serious.

'As for you Sherin, you know we all like you and we despised the way old Crew treated you, but we couldn't do nuthin' 'bout it. Maybe now it's time you got married and raised a family. That bounty hunter sitting next to you deserves a reward for plugging Crew.' He turned directly to Trey. 'We don't know nuthin' about you, mister, but we'd be happy for you to stick around.'

Trey smiled, Sherin blushed and looked away. Trey held up his hand to speak, but Sherin jumped in first. She stood up.

'Trey got sucked into all this without knowing just what he was getting into. You boys don't need to know what was going on but you probably know Irish, Indian and Gambini were sent to catch me after I ran off. I was trying to fathom out a fraud that Kerne was running and get him locked up and out of my life. I disguised myself as a Mexican 'cos it's not safe to be a

155

woman on your own out there. I was tracking down some silver. Most of you know I wanted to be rid of Kerne. I didn't necessarily want him to die but I wanted to be free and I was gathering evidence against him to put him away. Maybe he's better off dead. Trey here just happened to be in the right place at the wrong time, got caught up in some hot-headed action that shouldn't have happened, but he didn't deserve to hang, so, well anyway that's another story.' She paused and turned to Trey. 'I'd like you to stay on and help me run this place. Would you?'

The ranch hands banged the table loudly. Trey was put on the spot and he didn't like it. He turned to Sherin.

'I'll give you an answer in the morning.'

Unfortunately, ranch hands being what they were, misinterpreted his remark and all hell broke loose with whooping and laughing and disgustingly lewd comments about how he'd make up his mind. Sherin took the opportunity to break up the party.

'That's enough, boys! Get on out to the bunkhouse and wash your mouths out with soap!'

They got up from the table with much laughter and knowing looks, dispersing into the night. Trey and Sherin were left sitting at the table as cook came in to clear the dishes.

'I'm sorry for their behaviour,' Sherin said.

'You can't blame them for coming to the wrong conclusion.'

'Is it a wrong conclusion?' Sherin asked. 'Don't you want to spend the night with me?'

156

'And risk being drugged again!'

They both laughed, but Sherin was serious. 'Not just this night. Maybe they were right, it could be time for me to raise a family. I'll need a son to pass on the ranch when I'm too old to work it.'

Trey looked at her, then just as quickly dropped his gaze.

'That's a long way in the future. Look, today's been a bit of a day, one way and another. Hoss needs some oats. . . .'

'That's all taken care of, he's in the stable next to my palomino. He's being looked after.'

'Yeah, but . . . you know when we were out on the road, it was different. I slept in the chair, or tried to. This is kinda more personal, it's your home an' all that. It doesn't feel quite right to take the place of a man I just shot to death.'

'Kerne and I didn't sleep together, Trey. I wouldn't let him.'

'Sherin, like I said, I need to think this through and I'll give you an answer in the morning.'

Sherin put her arm round his shoulder and kissed his cheek.

There was one other thing on Trey's mind. One other reason to delay an answer.

'Have you got that account book and any other evidence? I have to take that to Corburg to wrap up this mission.'

'Let that go. There's no need to pursue it now Kerne's dead. The operation will come to a close. All you could do now is find out where the bars were

157

being doctored. That could take ages. Casey & Co will fold up without Kerne, and if it doesn't, somebody will shut it down one day. You don't need to go back to Corburg, there's enough money here in the ranch and the mining. Anyway, I'd like you to stay.'

Trey knew he had to confess something else, he had to be honest about the reward that was waiting in Corburg. It wasn't the financial reward. It was the job he'd set his heart on.

'In the morning,' he repeated. 'Now show me to a spare bed, please.'

If he thought he was going to drop into a dreamless sleep he was way off the mark. Sleep kept passing him by. Every time he thought his mind was cleared, images suddenly appeared to ward off refreshing oblivion. One moment it was Sherin, next it was the deputy's star, then the cell at Reeves Hope and Bud squashed against the bars at Copps Creek, next the sound of Irish snoring, and back to the night under the stars with Sherin so close yet so far.

He remained stubbornly awake.

He kept running over the events of the last few weeks, the judge and jury, the jails, the sheriffs, the deception, the escapes, the confusion. But above all those unpleasant things, there was one shining angel, one redeeming feature, one indescribable thrill – the racing of his heart when he thought of Sherin. But in the next moment he was wracked with doubt. Twenty-five was too young to be tied down in marriage, too young to be raising a family, too young for that kind of responsibility.

On the other hand, the thought of spending each day near to Sherin, and each night even closer, would not leave his mind without a fight. He struggled.

Eventually dawn threw a grey glow round the curtain, and in the next moment, perversely, he was fast asleep.

When he woke, Trey's mind felt clear. He threw back the curtain and the sun streamed in through the window. He stood there for a moment and looked out at the pasture rolling away into the distance towards the forest and the far off Rockies. He would have to go out to the woods, clear his camp and collect his things. He splashed his face with water from the jug, later he would have hot water for a shave, right now the smell of bacon was wafting through the house.

Sherin was already at the table drinking coffee. Her hair was gleaming like polished copper and neatly tied back in a ponytail ready for the morning ride. Her green eyes met Trey's with a warm smile, but she was nervously waiting for his decision.

'Coffee? Ready to ride out? Have you made up your mind?'

'Too many questions,' he replied. 'I'm not awake until I've had my coffee.'

Breakfast passed in polite, but hesitant, chat. The atmosphere was tense, there was a lot of hope and expectations flying around. They hung like clouds hiding the sun while full of rain; which would prevail, the sun or the rain?

'Let's ride,' Sherin said, getting up from the table. 'We can ride the boundary, I want to show you the land.'

They walked out to the stable together and saddled up. Trey was glad to see Hoss looking fit and well. He pulled his ears and said something quietly to the mustang. Hoss gave him an odd look in return.

Leading the horses out into the yard, Trey and Sherin each felt the day had something good in store. They climbed into the saddles. The sun was up, the grass was green, the men were at work. Everything was good. What more was there to enjoy in life? Before they left the yard, Sherin couldn't help herself.

'Trey, have you made a decision? Tell me.'

'Yes,' he said. 'I have.'

Before he could say any more, Sherin had spurred the palomino and raced off.

Hoss stamped impatiently on the ground. If only horses could talk! *Do we catch her or let her go?*